THE BATH SHORT STORY AWARD ANTHOLOGY 2016

THE BATH SHORT STORY AWARD ANTHOLOGY 2016

Compiled by
Jude Higgins, Jane Riekemann
and Anna Schlesinger

BROWN
DOG
BOOKS

Published under licence by Brown Dog Books and
The Self-Publishing Partnership
7 Green Park Station, Bath BA1 1JB

www.selfpublishingpartnership.co.uk

ISBN printed book: 978-1-78545-127-0
ISBN e-book: 978-1-78545-128-7

Cover design by Elinor Nash
Book internal design by Andrew Easton

Printed and bound by CPI Group (UK) Ltd, Croydon CR0 4YY

CONTENTS

INTRODUCTION

The Bath Short Story Award is firmly established in the international literary calendar and we're excited to publish our fourth anthology this year. The twenty stories in this book were shortlisted for the award, displaying writing styles that vary from poetic prose to more traditional structures. Contemporary and historic themes and a range of genres, including the increasingly popular magical realism, form the backbone of these narratives.

It was not easy to choose a shortlist out of the 1439 entries we received from all over the world (45 countries to be precise) with a wealth of subject matter that enlightened, amused and moved us to tears – occasionally within the same story. The common denominator was the human experience and the things that affect us all. Therefore, we had stories about poverty, disability, ageing, childhood memories, relationships between friends, families and lovers and, inevitably, there were several variations on the refugee theme. So many choices, but in the end what makes a memorable story is the telling of it.

Once again we worked with a team of ten readers, all active writers, to produce a longlist out of which emerged the shortlist

– selected by us. We were delighted that Bristol-based BBC Radio 4 producer Mair Bosworth agreed to choose the winners and her comments on the three winning and three commended stories can be read in the authors' profiles.

Many writers on the short and longlists are already successful so, to give those who are unpublished a second chance, we award the Acorn prize. The Local Prize, chosen by us, is donated by Nic Bottomley of Mr B's Emporium of Books in Bath and we thank him for all his support.

This year we widened our activities by inviting novelist Paul McVeigh to present his sell-out 'Killer First Page' workshop in Bath Library and we hosted a lively evening of readings with local authors. We also work closely with Bath Flash Fiction Award.

We hope you enjoy these stories; their authors come from the United Kingdom, the United States, New Zealand, Ireland, Luxembourg and Belgium and provide a varied and rich reading experience. If they inspire you to write, the 2017 Bath Short Story Award opens in November with details on our website www.bathshortstoryaward.org

Jude Higgins, Jane Riekemann and Anna Schlesinger
Follow us on Twitter @BathStoryAward

Subscribe on the site to receive news and updates on the competition.

ACKNOWLEDGEMENTS

The Bath Short Story Award is a team effort and, once again, we were supported by our dedicated and enthusiastic readers. Each story was read by two people from the team who recommended their favourites for the longlist. For the 2016 award we thank:

Anne Corlett
Jo Derrick
Fiona Longsdon
Val Mote
Jonathan Pinnock
Katharina Riekemann
Pat Robson
Diane Simmons
Simon Toseland
Alison Woodhouse

Once again, our thanks go to Mr B's Emporium of Reading Delights, Bath www.mrbsemporium.com for donating the Local Prize. An award winning independent bookshop with quirky décor and an eclectic range of books, it's become the traditional venue for our anthology launches in the autumn.

The 2014 BSSA was won by local writer and artist Elinor Nash www.elenash.com who has continued to provide our artwork ever since. This year's cover is an adaptation of her original stunning design and we are so grateful for her support.

2016 JUDGE
MAIR BOSWORTH

We were thrilled to welcome Mair Bosworth as our shortlist judge for 2016. Mair is based in Bristol, where she produces Book at Bedtime, short stories, poetry programmes and arts documentaries for BBC Radio 4. She has broadcast work by Kazuo Ishiguro, William Boyd, Owen Sheers, Kate Clanchy and AL Kennedy. Kit de Waal's story 'The Beautiful Thing' which won our second prize in 2014 was also produced by her. Mair runs the Bristol branch of 'In the Dark', a collective of radio producers and enthusiasts, which celebrates the best of radio storytelling. Mair's comments on the commended and winning entries can be read at the end of the authors' biographies, but there are some more general observations below. You can follow Mair on Twitter at @heyheymaimai

'When I agreed to be the shortlist judge for this year's Bath Short Story Award, I didn't know what a hard task I was taking on. I have been really impressed with the shortlisted stories and would like to congratulate everyone who got this far in the competition. Picking a top three has not been easy. Reading these stories I have been transported to Brooklyn, Tangier, Dublin, Appalachia, Bangor. I have encountered some startling, imaginative storytelling and some brilliantly drawn characters who have really stuck with me. There is great energy and originality in these stories, matched with control and craft. Thank you to everyone who sent in their stories – it's been an honour to read them all.'

FIRST PRIZE
ANNE O'BRIEN

Feather Your Nest

I cup an egg and knock it against the rim of the bowl. The white slithers out dragging the yolk behind it. It spreads out at the bottom. Declan flips bacon. His hairy legs stick out of his worn dressing gown, incongruous, like the homely smell of frying bacon in the too quiet kitchen.

'They've put a "For Sale" sign up next door,' I say.

Silence.

'Maybe the new people will do something about the garden.'

Declan loads his plate and sits at the kitchen table. He props the newspaper against the milk jug and places his new reading glasses low on his nose.

'Do you think we could lop the pine trees before someone notices?'

'Pine trees?'

'Next door...'

'Trees like that, you'd need a permit.'

'It wouldn't have mattered before. You'd have just gone in with the chainsaw.'

'Don't start...'

I look at our garden, at the neat flower beds bordering the unused lawn. I fight the urge to scratch the patches of eczema on my hands.

The bells of the nearby convent ring out and I think of the nuns, up since dawn, the hours of their day parcelled up by the summons to pray.

'Maybe we should get a dog,' I say. 'Now would be a good time, before new neighbours move in.'

'What?'

'A labrador maybe?'

'Think of the mess.'

I look out at row of triangles made by the bamboo canes supporting the sweetpeas.

'Better get dressed.' Declan pushes back his chair. 'Squash with Mike. I'll be back around one.'

I take my coffee into the living room and switch on the telly. The screen flickers to life. A man in a tweed suit stands in an aviary, explaining how to treat an egg-bound bird. I reach for the remote control averting my eyes from the close-up of the canary's fierce swollen bottom and the magnified tip of a cotton bud dipped in oil. *Zoowatch*, flick, *Homes Under the Hammer*, flick, *Desperate Housewives*, off, then silence.

A steady stream of people view the house. There are parents towing reluctant teenagers.

'Imagine the noise,' says Declan.

Then a young couple, the wife's pregnant belly pushing out her sweatshirt.

'They'd be better,' he says. But all I think are the small animal cries of a newborn coming through the adjoining wall and I know I couldn't bear it.

Finally, a couple of professionals, in their late 30s.

I make scones the day they move in, after a two month renovation project. I cut each one in half, top them with a blob of raspberry jam and cream and arrange them on my best plate. I knock on the newly painted front door.

'Hi, I'm Isabelle, from next door.' I hand the plate to a short round woman in a yellow cotton dress. She has a head of prematurely grey curls.

'I'm Liz,' she says. 'Come on in, I've just put the kettle on.' She leads me down a sunny hallway smelling of beeswax. It seems wrong to keep my shoes on so I slip them off. The parquet feels silky under my feet. I follow her into the kitchen with its cream cupboards and gleaming Aga.

After coffee, she gives me a tour of the house. I like the master bedroom best. The gold and rubies of the Klimt 'Kiss' over the bed are picked up by the burnt orange of a kilim rug. We look out on the two gardens, one so neat, the other, a dark tangle of trees and undergrowth.

'We'll start on ours soon. We wanted to ask you, would you mind if we took down the pines?'

The thought of the sunlight streaming into our garden makes me giddy. Maybe this year the tomatoes will ripen. Declan is as pleased as I am. I tell him all about their house; the light, the colours, the wooden floors... I want to rush through ours, pulling up carpets and sweeping designer junk into black plastic bags. But all I say is,

'Maybe I'll re-paint the bedroom.'

'Remember, the doctor said, you need rest to get over the breakdown.'

'"Burnout", Declan. That's what it's called, "Burnout".'

'Whatever.' His eyes slide away. I feel the fear in him, that I'll stay cooped up in this house and never get better, or maybe that I will get better and leave him, walk right out the door in search of a new mate.

I want to scream, 'Thirty-seven. I'm only thirty-seven. There's still time...'

But I'm silenced by the way the thinning crown of his head bends over the crossword.

True to Liz's word, a couple of weeks go by and then they start. A team of gardeners transforms the wilderness. The pine trees are felled, their branches fed to a machine that spits out wood chip. Rolls of turf are unfurled and the ivy covered ground is replaced by a green carpet watered by a sprinkler that twists and turns making miniature rainbows. A new lavender hedge beside the fence already hums with bees. They lay a woodchip path from the back door. It meanders through the velvet grass leading nowhere, until a few days later when, early one morning, a brown van pulls up.

Two good looking lads, with not a hint of a builder's bottom between them, emerge. They carry in equipment, high on their broad shoulders. Tools dangle from leather belts slung on their hips.

I watch them dig foundations and then build a garden shed, laying one plank of honey coloured wood against another. The gravelly voice of Leonard Cohen singing 'I'm Your Man' comes from the ghetto blaster they hang on the fence. Their voices drift into our kitchen.

'Sand that one down, Tom. Can't have anyone getting splinters.' They laugh, their handsome heads thrown back.

Liz appears, carrying a tray with three mugs clustered together and one of those fancy coffee plunger things. She's at home these days, like me, but then again, maybe not.

I don't remember much from my last day at work. Declan says someone from the medical service talked me out of the ladies loo where I'd barricaded myself. I'd forgotten that. He says I should 'take it easy'. And do what? Mornings are the worst, the day ahead just too big to face. I usually close my eyes and try to sink back into sleep.

Liz drinks coffee with them in the garden. I hear them chatter and the roll of her laughter. She eats lunch with them too. In the afternoons she serves tea from a china teapot – I'm sure it's Earl Grey. Once the walls are up, they bring their tea inside and close the shed door behind them.

After three days they pack up, carrying out left-over wood, their tool belts swinging, dark sweat stains on their t-shirts. Liz's partner Rebecca is home early. She's in the garden with Liz. The breeze makes tufts of her short auburn hair.

I start on a cheese soufflé for dinner. Separating eggs, I toss the golden ball of yolk from one shell to the other letting the whites slip down into the bowl.

The next time I look, Becks has her arm around Liz's shoulders and they're both looking at the shed. It looks like it's always been there, a little mountain cabin nestled in the grass. The door is propped open and I see the gleam of the polished wood of two deep shelves running high along both walls.

Once the soufflé's in the oven, I check again. They're facing each other now, lifting their arms and then bending at the waist until their heads almost touch the grass. Again and again they stretch, drawing closer to the shed until they go inside.

A few moments pass, then Becks emerges, goes into the house and returns with her arms full of cushions. Liz moves around the shed, stroking the wood with her plump hand. She places the cushions in two piles on one of the high shelves. Then they clamber up and sit on them, their heads almost touching the roof and their feet dangling clear off the floor.

I'm bursting to tell Declan but when he gets home he immediately starts flicking his phone saying there's some crisis at work. The soufflé flops; I scrape the brown rubbery mess into the bin.

Instead, I pour two large glasses of Chardonnay and take out cheese, olives, and a loaf of bread; the kind of meal we had when we first moved in. But after a couple of minutes, Declan pushes his plate away, saying he's got to send off some emails. As I brush my teeth before bed I look out the window. It's the first real summer's night and there's a warm glow from the shed. The door is propped open and I can see Becks and Liz perched side by side on the high bench.

Early next morning, I check again. They're still there, their heads drooping low on their chests. I think I hear them gently snoring.

Three days go by and they seldom leave the shed. Declan is away at a conference so I make a big pot of soup and sit and watch them. The second night, I doze in an armchair, pulled up close to the patio doors in the kitchen. It's as though I'm waiting for something to happen. And then, on the third day, just as the convent bells ring out 8am, it does.

The dew shimmers as Liz and Becks dance barefoot on the grass.

I have to find out what's going on so I waylay the postman, 'Anything for number 25?' I say. 'They're away.' My luck is in and he hands me a lumpy parcel, squishy to touch.

I ring their doorbell, but there's no answer, so I go around the side entrance.

They come out of the shed to greet me, smiling and reaching out to stroke my angora cardigan. Their cheeks are rosy and their hair messy. I feel the warmth of their hands through my sleeve. I thrust the parcel at them.

'A mix up? It's from Mothercare.'

They rip open the wrapping and lift out one babygro after another, creamy white, pale yellow... The tiny clothes make my insides stretch with longing. I think of all the little clothes in mothballs in a suitcase in our attic.

'But...?'

'Shush,' says Liz. 'Come and see.'

Inside the shed, dappled sunlight picks out the vivid colours of the cushions and a few stray feathers. The air is full of the drowsy smell of sun-warmed wood. My eyes adjust and follow her gaze. They come to rest on a large brown speckled egg lying in the centre of a cushion.

All I can think of are the summers I spent with Granny; how I'd crouch and go into the hens' coop to fetch eggs for breakfast. Watching their fierce eyes and the bright red of their wattles, I'd move closer and slide my hand under their hot bodies. I'd carry warm eggs back to the kitchen as the squawks died down and dusty peace descended.

'Well?' says Liz.

This egg is bigger than a hen's egg, bigger even than the pale blue duck eggs we used to find in their haphazard nests amongst reeds by the pond. My fingers long to hold it, to feel the tiny spark of life pulsing inside it.

'How lovely,' I say.

Liz and Becks climb back up on the benches. Liz eases her ample bottom over the egg. Becks pushes a couple of cushions along and I climb up beside them. I hear the soft thud as my sandals hit the floor. My body swells and settles, my breasts pushing against the downy wool of my cardigan.

The day passes in a sleepy blur, peace seeping through to the marrow of my bones. Night falls before I think to stir and only then because I hear the bells calling the nuns to evening prayer and I remember that I have to pick Declan up from the train.

As I leave, Liz pushes a small card into my hand, closing my fingers over it; its sharp edges prick my palm.

I spot Declan getting down from the last carriage. There is something in the way he tosses his backpack over his shoulder that takes me back to our student days. I watch him walk, thin on top, but loose limbed and easy. I raise my hand and he waves back.

We make love that night, for the first time in months. Afterwards, when his breath comes slow and regular and his arm lies heavy across my belly, I ease myself out and tiptoe to the bathroom. I pick up my jeans and a small card drops onto the white tiles. Taking it to the window, I read by the light of a full moon,

Call Tom and Eric to feather your nest
Let us turn your house into a home.

I tuck the card at the back of the bathroom cabinet.

Maybe next spring. I can wait until then. But next spring, if nothing's happened, I'll get the garden shed sorted.

Anne O'Brien left her job in the European Commission in Brussels five years ago to pursue her passion in creative writing. Since then, she has gained a Masters degree in Creative Writing at Lancaster University and is currently working towards her PhD. Her stories have been shortlisted in many competitions the Sunday Business Post/Penguin Ireland Short Story competition, the Bridport Prize, BBC's Opening Lines and the Fish Short Story Prize. Anne's work has appeared in several anthologies and magazines as well, and has been translated and published in Vietnamese.

Mair Bosworth commented:

'Impressive in its clarity and control of tone and language, this is a quiet, poised story that holds great emotion just beneath the surface. Apparently simple and unadorned, I relished the startling shift that happens midway through this story, when the reader is taken somewhere else entirely. The egg symbolism could have felt clunky in another writer's hands, but here it was used sensitively and effectively to speak about fertility, loss and hope. I loved the sparing use of painful details: the quiet kitchen, the baby clothes in the attic, the claustrophobia of daytime TV and the pines casting their shadow across the garden. This story hooked me right away and charmed, moved and surprised me. It is a worthy winner.'

SECOND PRIZE

BARRY McKINLEY

Almost Home

The Oscar Wilde ferry rested in the Wexford harbour with its engines idling. The photographer sent by the State asked Slattery and Tarrant to step out of the picture. The big men shuffled aside, leaving Ali framed by the heavy doors at the back of the ship. The photographer used a flash, even though the day was bright. Ali gave his famous cheesy grin and two thumbs up to the man with the Nikon.

'I want say thank you to Ireland.'

The photographer turned away to fill out the details in his notebook.

'I have so happy in Ireland. Many times happy. People good. Weather good. Guinness good...'

Tarrant scowled and said, 'Give it a rest.' He knew that Mahfouz spoke perfect English and this endless act was beginning to annoy him.

Slattery had the tickets and passports in a zipped pouch. He also had papers that identified their status as private contractors, signed by the Minister himself. In another pouch, plastic tie handcuffs, for use in extreme circumstances. Force would be a last resort.

The photographer got into his Audi and drove away. The men walked up the sloping steel roadway, Slattery on the left, Tarrant on the right, and Ali Mahfouz dwarfed in the middle. From the rear, he looked like a small child going on holiday with a pair of muscular uncles.

The cabin had four bunks, a dressing table and a tiny bathroom. The room hummed as the turbine spun in the space below their feet. There was no porthole. The air was fresh, but unmoving. The bed sheets were clean and the towels neatly folded. It was quite pleasant, overall, and Ali nodded his approval.

'We're travellin' in style, boys,' he said. 'We're on a mighty journey.'

Slattery laughed, but Tarrant just sniffed his disapproval. He blocked Ali into a corner and barked in a South London accent, peppered with words a foreigner might not easily understand.

'Alright, sunshine. A few pointers. You be a good boy and we'll treat you right. Any hanky-panky... We're not coppers, comprendo? I can and I will smack you, and if I smack you, you will remember it.' Tarrant produced the plastic cuffs. He held them up like a flight attendant explaining safety procedures. 'Start playing silly buggers, this is what you get.'

Ali slipped off his shoes and climbed the ladder to an upper bunk. He lay down and looked at the ceiling tiles.

He was seventeen when he arrived in Ireland, and he made friends everywhere, instantly. He told people he was a medical student and his Facebook picture showed an eager young man standing outside the College of Surgeons with a bundle of books – two of which were telephone directories. His youth carried him through the first couple of years. The men he met on George's Street were mostly kind. They gave him gifts and allowed him to sleep on their sofas. Back then, in the Tiger years, everybody had money. A professor in Trinity College gave him two hundred Euros and urged him to buy a ticket back to Tangier, but he bought an iPod instead. He walked around Dublin with the little white buds tucked into his ears, even though he never learned how to load the device with music.

The ship rose and fell and Ali considered how much rain it would take to fill an ocean. That was the thing he liked most about Ireland. The rain. The way it lashed down and swept around you in circles. Moroccan rain had the light touch of tiny baby fingers, but Irish rain was a smack from an open hand, a watery assault, a fight in liquid form.

Every now and then Ali looked over the edge of his bunk to see Tarrant slowly turning the pages on a Buy & Sell magazine, occasionally circling advertisements with a red pen.

Ali thought of the jobs he had done during his stay in Ireland. He had worked for two Egyptian brothers, slicing kebab meat into a half-moon pan. He had power-washed cars, scrubbed pots and wiped down tables. He had sold Christmas trees, door to door, in November and for eighteen months he worked in the meatpacking plant where he picked up the best of his Irish expressions:

'Soft day, tough shite and did your Mammy make any more like you?'

Eventually he slept and, when he awoke, Tarrant and Slattery were moving around the cabin, preparing for disembarkation.

'Wakey-wakey!'

'Eggs and bakey,' Ali replied.

Slattery laughed, but Tarrant remained stony faced, as always.

It was nine hours later when Ali made his first attempt at escape. They were in a service station somewhere near Bordeaux, eating limp sandwiches and drinking Orangina.

Ali jumped up and ran to a nearby table where a small

intense woman picked at her food. 'Help me,' he begged her in French, 'these men are foreign soldiers and they have abducted me on French soil. Somebody must help me.'

'Get back here,' Tarrant demanded.

'Is this true?' The woman asked.

Slattery wiped his mouth with a serviette, smiled at the woman, and then spoke in perfect French.

'Madame, we are legally deporting this man from the Republic of Ireland. We have made two previous attempts to remove him from our country by air but, on each occasion, he was disruptive and alarmed the other passengers by calling out, 'I am a jihadi. I have a bomb and I will blow up this plane.'

Ali gave the woman a broad smile, which she did not return. Slattery continued.

'If you feel we are doing anything that contravenes French law, you must of course contact the local gendarmerie. We will hand this man over to their custody, and he will become your responsibility.' Slattery put heavy emphasis on 'votre responsabilité.' The woman frowned. Ali gave her a hopeful two thumbs up, but she just shook her head and returned to her cold ravioli.

In the car, Tarrant caught Ali's attention in the rear-view mirror; he growled like a dog. Slattery took the handcuffs out of his pouch and tied Ali's wrists together.

'Your French is very good,' Ali said.

'Thank you,' Slattery replied.

Ali studied the Irishman and noticed he wasn't wearing a wedding band, though he was probably in his mid-thirties and quite handsome. There was always the possibility that they had crossed paths on George's Street, but Slattery's eyes gave nothing away.

Ali's second escape attempt occurred when he requested a bathroom stop just south of Salamanca. They pulled into a *Tangerina* and parked under a giant sign that said 'Autogrill'. An articulated truck rumbled past as they walked across the wide concrete forecourt. In an instant, Ali ducked down and dashed under the body of the trailer, barely dodging the moving wheels. He ran, his hands still bound, with no idea where he was going. He zigzagged around parked cars and squeezed through the tight spaces between tourist buses. A towbar caught him in the shin; the pain was instant and crippling. He hobbled around the back of a bright yellow furniture van and ran straight into Tarrant's fist, a wall made of bone and skin. He crumpled to the gravel in agony; Tarrant stood over him, cursing.

'Sneaky little bastard!'

Ali licked his lips and tasted blood. Slattery said, 'Easy now,' and it wasn't entirely clear to whom he was speaking.

The burnt scrub of southern Spain was slowly lost to the night. Ali stared sideways out the window, and watched the cars crawl past in the fast lane. Tarrant slept beside him, like a best friend leaning in for comfort, his head resting on Ali's shoulder. The journey was almost over, two more hours by road to Tarifa, and then thirty minutes on the ferry to Tangier. Ali spoke to himself, and indirectly, to Slattery.

'In Tangier, ten years ago, they caught me in bed with another boy. Half his right foot was missing... a Mobylette accident, you know, but apart from that he was quite beautiful. They brought him to the prison in Sidi Moussa and beat him with steel rods. He lost an eye and most of his teeth.'

Slattery glanced in the mirror.

'They will bring me to the same place,' Ali said.

'We have assurances from your government,' Slattery replied.

Ali smiled. 'You should know by now you can't trust a Moroccan.'

Tarrant made a snorting noise and burrowed deeper into Ali's shoulder. The dark sky ripped in places and lightness showed through. Slattery turned on the air conditioner, to catch the morning heat before it started.

'Did I tell you my theory about Ireland?' Ali asked.

Slattery shook his head.

'Ireland is like the man who invites people to his house for a feast, and then discovers he does not have enough food. He tries to hide his humiliation with anger. He shouts and curses at his guests and forces them out into the night.'

'You weren't a guest,' Slattery said, 'You were an illegal alien.'

At 11am, the three men stood on the deck of a high-speed ferry that cut the Mediterranean like a scissors through cloth. Slattery had wiped the blood from Ali's chin with a paper towel, but the plastic cuffs remained in place.

'Bloody hot,' Tarrant said, making no attempt to remove his jacket.

The journey was so quick, it felt more like a river than a sea crossing. The white hill of houses, cut by a band of trees, rose up over the horizon.

'Tangier!' Tarrant reacted as if he had been expecting somewhere else.

Slattery patted Ali on the shoulder and said, 'Almost home.'

Ali thought about his mother and sisters and the cramped apartment in Beni Makada. How they raised two thousand Euros just to spirit him out of the country, and how he never paid a cent of it back. It was shameful. And now, three years in jail ahead of him. Food, clothing and bribes, how much more money would they have to find to save him from being eaten alive?

'Almost,' Ali said, raising his cuffed hands to give his companions two thumbs up. 'Almost.'

The smile was still on Ali's lips when he vaulted the railing. He hung in the air for a moment before accelerating downwards, his thumbs still pointing upwards. A woman screamed, a crew member raised the alarm and the ship's engines stopped. Slattery and Tarrant rushed to the rail and looked over. There was no sign of Ali.

Underwater, the world was quiet. The shadow cast by the boat overhead looked like a dark cloud on a grey sky. Some tiny fish seemed inquisitive; they circled the falling man for a moment and then departed.

The strength of the water surprised Ali, the way it pulled him down; he couldn't fight it even if he wanted to. He wondered how long it would hold him under; would it be for hours or days? Would it eventually toss him on a sandy beach or would it pull him into the stream that endlessly circles the earth. He swallowed a mouthful and then he swallowed some more. It didn't taste that bad and it reminded him of something, something that made him smile – if you closed your eyes, it was just like Irish rain.

Barry McKinley was nominated in 2010 for Best New Play, Irish Theatre Awards (for *Elysium Nevada*). He has written plays for BBC Radio 4 and RTE. His stories were twice shortlisted for the Hennessy Literary Award. His forthcoming memoir, *It Ends With Blood,* will be published in 2017.

Mair Bosworth commented:

'Of all the stories I read, this is perhaps the one that has stuck with me most vividly. I loved its humour, set against the dark reality of its subject matter. I loved its relentless pace and action, driving the narrative towards the emotional kick of its inevitable conclusion. I felt instantly attached to the characters (who are drawn with skill and affection) and there is some great, cinematic, imagery (Ali, for example, watching the cars pass on the motorway as the 'burnt scrub of southern Spain was slowly lost to the night'). I was impressed by the sense of intimacy created between the three men at the heart of the story: uneasy travelling companions locked together in fulfilment of the unpleasant task at hand; an unlikely trio, framed in the tight spaces of a ferry cabin, a car, a doorway. 'Almost Home' is an impassioned story of great warmth and humanity that manages to stay the right side of sugary. It puts a human face to one of the great challenges of our present time and is a good read to boot.'

THIRD PRIZE
SARA COLLINS

Say You

That summer was the summer of R&B and slow rock and dancehall. Lionel Richie topped the charts and we spent weekends grinding to *Say you, say me*, cheek to shoulder with the home-grown boys who fingered the buttons on our jeans. We craved bubble skirts and denim jackets and the lipsticks we saw in *Cosmo* magazine. We wanted American style and American food and the lives of girls played by Molly Ringwald in American movies.

It was the best of times, as the saying goes.

And then the Cubanos arrived.

The first girl to snag one was Jewel Remedios, named after her grandmother, from whom she'd inherited penny-coloured hair that spilled over her shoulders like melting butter, dark eyebrows and a full-cheeked face that crisped up in the sun as quickly as the edges of a frying egg. We envied her all of this – that much goes without saying – and Jewel Remedios lived for nothing if not to be envied.

They'd arrived in July, some in sailboats measled with paint, others in swollen shark coloured rafts crawling along the corrugated shoreline. They were headed for Miami. Nothing really existed in between. Nothing they were interested in. They didn't want to stop, only hollered for water, waving their plastic bottles and pointing at their stomachs. Behind them, the cruise ships drifted indifferently, as clean and white as jawbones.

The story of any island is basically the story of men, arriving. Where are the women in the history of the new world? Waiting for that first glimpse of strangers riddled with chin-fur and sailors' itch, pale as worms, bearing crappy gifts of beads and nails in the hope that it would be enough to *get* them nailed, the first thing they wanted after months at sea. Ha! Those women all tittered and giggled, every last one of them, their bellies full of laughter, but still they fell for it, every time: the promise of something different, something new.

The authorities pulled the Cubans ashore, moved them into camps.

We began to see them around town, the young ones on day passes, no older than nineteen, twenty. Damp with sweat and aftershave. They had a hunger on them, like seamen or jailbirds. Their eyes glinted like knife-blades. We wanted to see how close we could get.

Bienvenido, bienvenido, we said, nodding at them. Among ourselves, we started to talk like horny dockworkers. *Aiii, aii, aii I got a real boner for Mr Pretty Eyes* or *Mamacita, cool me down, I done see my last chance!*

They noticed us. Of course they did. We'd developed our own little careful swaggers, pulsing our hips in our cut-offs, T-shirts over one shoulder, rattling our bangles. We were Madonna, *circa* Like A Virgin. We strung ourselves like ching-ching birds along the low wall at the harbour. They stopped to ask for directions. We asked what Havana was like, spilling over into disciplined giggles.

Just before sunset, the boys raced back to camp for curfew, and we had no choice but to watch them go – our *Cinderellos* – knowing only that we wanted more from them than we had yet received.

Jewel started going off with Abel, a tall, quiet boy with a hard face whom the other boys called El Jefe.

Jewel's two best friends, Maxine and Sherry – the Stepsisters – reported to the rest of us, gleefully, that the first time Jewel and Abel did it, when she'd seen his *thing* poking out at her like a dowsing rod, she'd slid straight off the deckchair and thrown up all over his sneakers where he'd left them in the sand, but Abel, with the patience of a saint, had used his own T-shirt to clean her off, then whispered Spanish things in her ear that she couldn't understand but which felt like tiny little shocks that went through her all the way to her toes and, we imagined, right into what our grandmas would have called her lockbox.

After that, she started learning Spanish herself, feeding him her new words like tidbits from her own tongue: *Te amo, Abel, Te quiero, Abelito*.

His friends Carlito and Frederico paired up with Maxine and Sherry and, slowly but surely, we all found our own Cuban boys as the summer wore on.

It was mid-August, the height of hurricane season, the mangroves were swollen with rain, the mosquitoes buzzed mercilessly at our ears as we fell asleep, even on the evenings when the control planes droned overhead, or the pesticide truck heehawed past, spraying the bushes and fields. We taught the boys to play American drinking games like quarters and landmines and flip-up-cup, games that we ourselves had only seen on television, knowing that we were preparing them for their lives in Florida and away from us.

They told us about Havana: prostitutes strolling the Malecón; the cigar factories where workers had the newspapers read to them every morning and posters of Fidel and Che brooded from every wall, Fidel looking miserable, like always, because Che was *el guapo*, the panty thief, the martyr, the one who looked like an icon and had been frozen in time while he, Fidel, was just an aging bureaucrat. They told us about helping their *papas* build the boats before they left, in covered courtyards, in garages, in abandoned churches and sometimes in someone's living room – pushing everything aside to make room, knowing they risked prison if caught.

They worried that they wouldn't like Miami, after their parents had risked everyone's lives to get there. Then what?

Jewel took Abel for ice cream, to make out at the lighthouse, to climb along the ironshore and wait for water to splash them through the blowholes; some days she piled the rest of us in and we drove to the cliffs to watch the waves come in, waiting for the perfect one before we pushed ourselves up and away, out to the salt bite of the sea. We dried off lying on the grass, playing top 40 through the car radio. Jewel danced and pointed at Abel, wiggling her hips. *Say you…say me.* He smiled, but in a slightly bemused way.

Jewel began to probe and probe at him like an infected tooth. She wanted promises.

'*Flaquita,* no father want me for his little girl,' he said. 'I have nothing; I am nothing. The sea turned me, my whole family, into ghosts. Puff! We are nothing; we do nothing; we have nothing. We're in *purgatorio,* waiting for lives to start.'

'But this isn't nothing!' she protested waving her hands between them.

'It all feels like limbo,' he said. 'I need to know where life is going first.'

'We'll get to know each other and then, in time... You can have visitors, right? I can come to camp…'

'It's only been a couple months, *guapa,*' he replied, running his hands over his close-cropped hair.

Carlos and Frederico took us aside, told us to tell her to cool it.

'I can't *cool* it,' she said.

One afternoon, after she had stormed off somewhere, we cornered Abel.

'How to explain to her? We are having a good summer, yes. Some fun. After that journey…but she and I, we are not in the same worlds! Our question is how to find a home, *make* one. On a stinking, leaking boat, in a tent, in *here*.' He pointed at his head. 'Your only question is where next to have fun. But this is not an American movie! She is *here*,' he smacked his hand on the sand, 'and I am there!' He swept his arm out in the direction of the ocean.

It was the most we'd ever heard him say at one time.

'*Cálmate*, Jefe,' his friends said.

Jewel's cheeks began to look pinched, she lost weight, she couldn't keep down anything but Supligen and curried goat, and her eyes gleamed as we sat by the ocean mourning the boys each night after they went back to camp.

She decided to go and see him. We couldn't talk her out of it.

We parked in the dusty lot just outside the fence, which was littered with government trucks and tarpaulin shelters where immigration officers sat counting forms. Row after row of khaki tents; the only colour from the clothes fluttering like bright flags and the listless garbage stacked at the gate. We smelled barbecued beef and the raw tang of several hundred humans being human.

'Orincon,' the officer said, a large, black woman with deep grooves down her cheeks and around her eyes. She ran her pen down rows of names. 'O-R-I-N-C-O-N. Nope. No Abel Orincon. No one processed in here in that name.'

'No, no, check again,' said Jewel, smiling as if she was afraid to change her expression. She stood unmoving while her hair flapped around her face.

The officer sniffed and made a show of looking again.

'No one.'

'Well, can we just go in, look around for him?' Maxine asked, putting her arm around Jewel's shoulders, excited by this turn of events. Jewel was becoming a tragic figure right before our eyes, someone who, finally, finally, was worthy of the way we had worshipped her all along.

'Against the rules. You have to be met, right here, see, by the person you're visiting, sign in, and back here within two hours to exit.'

'Can't you send someone to call him?'

'Look,' the officer closed the file with a snap. 'I don't know what business you girls think you have here, but *this*, this little love story you think you have going on, is a tale as old as time. These guys –'

Jewel took off, her sandals flying off behind her, cutting her feet on the gravel. The officer made a *steups* noise and fell back into her plastic chair. She looked around the rest of us. 'You girls can't learn. Never. I sorry for you.'

It was a long walk around the fence. The rest of us shaded our eyes with our hands. Jewel squinted defiantly and unwaveringly into the sun. The men from the camp rushed to pull and rattle the chain links as we walked by, their open shirts fluttering around their bare chests: *Tssss, baby! Who you looking for? Abel? Abel? I don't know no Abel, baby, but you can know me.*

'I'm going to call her Joya, if she's a girl,' Jewel announced, wearily. She looked defiant, and unconvinced. She hooked two fingers through the fence. One of the men, with the weathered face of an octogenarian and the gap-toothed smile of a nine year old, put two of his own fingers over hers and whistled. 'This is love, baby, true love. Beginning of sexy friendship,' he said, pursing his lips at her and making a kissing noise.

'Do you know Abel Orincon?' she said. "*Conoces Abel?'*

'Abel…?' he screwed up his face. 'I think so, *sí*.'

'You do?' she cried. 'Can you take us to him? Is he here?'

'You're looking at him, baby!' he pointed to himself and cackled.

A heavy truck loaded with plastic water bottles thundered by, showering us with dirt. 'I'm thirsty,' one of the Stepsisters grumbled. No one paid her any mind.

It was as if we could feel the melancholy weight of the dying day. Jewel's steps slowed and her mood wavered as the shadows began to come in. She slipped a scarf from her purse and over her head, stretched both arms out, and held on to the fence with her head bowed. She curled her bleeding toes into the dirt.

'Wait,' said Sherry. 'Wait.' She tried to yank Jewel away from the fence, but it was too late.

'Is that…?'

'Oh my God, oh my God.'

'Abel! Abel!'

There was a slight stiffening of his back, nothing you'd have seen if you weren't looking for it. He turned away from us, holding up the flap of a tent with one hand and a baby with the other. He ducked his head.

A short, curvy woman and a little girl, maybe two, three years old, came out of the tent. The little girl bounced up and down, galloping around him, through his legs and under the guy line. She had thin legs, knees like lightbulbs. Finally, she stopped and held up her hands, wanting to be lifted.

'Papa! Papa!' she said.

Sherry popped her gum and whistled. 'Oh shit.' We all looked over at Jewel, who rattled the fence and then hooked her hands and feet into it, climbing so she could be higher up when she called out his name, so you couldn't miss her unless you were trying to. But her shouts disappeared into the long tail of dust kicked up by a sudden wind.

Inside the camp, he crouched to kiss his little girl, who danced away into the dust ribbon.

Maxine put her hand on Jewel's calf. None of us said a word. Jewel looked down at us and we looked up at her. And we knew that, whoever that man was, Abel was someone we'd invented. He was just a boy made from summer, and to summer he had returned.

Sara Collins studied law at the London School of Economics and worked as a lawyer for seventeen years. She is a final year student for the Master of Studies in Creative Writing at Cambridge University, where she was the recipient of the 2015 Michael Holroyd Prize for Re-creative Writing. Her work has been published in the *2015 Bath Short Story Award Anthology* and in *The Caribbean Writer.* She is working on her debut novel, *Frannie Langton,* which was shortlisted for the 2016 Lucy Cavendish Fiction Prize. Twitter: @mrsjaneymac

Mair Bosworth commented:

'Brilliant. Refreshing and bold; a story with a swagger to match that of its characters. Great storytelling; alive with colour, pulsing with the energy of precocious teenage girl desire. I loved the way that the (apparent) invincibility of youth is set against details which unsettle the reader and hint at something more sinister behind this carefree summer: the indifferent cruise ships 'clean and white as jawbones', the 'shark coloured rafts', eyes 'glinting like knife-blades'. Some standout lines too: "The story of any island is basically the story of men, arriving". The story deftly handles the complex power dynamics between the young women and their Cubano 'Cinderellos'. I was left wanting more: as in the story, this is a summer that sticks forever.'

LOCAL PRIZE

ALISON POWELL

Who Said the River was Red?

We were only playing.

This was our excuse for everything that ever raised a wail. It was no excuse at all. It meant we knew full well that we were being mean, or that we'd pushed a person to the fine-lined edge of their limits. There'd be tears, for sure. Or in this case, no tears at all, just bright red guilty faces that got hotter as we ran from the river and up through the woods and then scattered across the estate, never to play there again.

I was only playing. You were only playing. We were only playing.

We conjugated our excuses, though in truth we were too young and wild to care a toss for form.

I'm still trying to correct myself.

I was only playing. You was only playing. We was only running for our lives, running from the blood that spewed along the middle of the river.

I might say it was artistic now. There was a programme on

the telly with a man who made a line of leaves and floated them along a stream. They told us it was art and I agreed. I wonder what the man would have to say of this.

The boy wasn't one of us. That was the thing.

Where we were dark and scrappy, he was blonde and clean and neat. I thought that if I licked his cheek he'd taste the way that Maccy's Sweet Shop smelled, all pink sherbet dust and sugar. Even from across the river I could swear I caught his scent. A pretty smell that didn't know what rivers meant. He wore grey shorts and socks that came up to his knees and a cap that was made of felt and had a bright red button on the top. Gabe, or maybe Wes, or Bev or perhaps it was me, but one of us, somebody said it was his switch.

'He's not a real boy. They turn him on in the morning and turn him off again at night. Don't they? Hey? I'm talking to you. Don't they turn you off at night?'

He didn't talk. He stood on the other side of the river while we flung ourselves about like cats.

'What's wrong with him?' asked Bev, or Wes, or Gabe, swinging fast and hard on the rope from where we stood, then off again across the water, their legs stretched out towards the boy. 'What's wrong with you?'

We had never seen his face before. And we were the lords of the river. We were the ones who flung the rope up over the tree, a rock tied to the end for weight and we'd shimmied up the trunk to wrap the rope around. We'd pinched the tyre from Bev's father's allotment and we'd sliced it in half with Frenchie Thomas's saw in the back of his oily old garage. We'd tied the knots and tested them, piling on together, swinging out across the water: one, two, three at a time to make sure it was firm.

It was 1962. Can you believe that now? 1962 and still we cannot hold each other's gaze.

He sat down in the long river grass and watched us for a while. We pretended we'd lost interest, became too busy swinging or rubbing sticks together to make fire.

'Keep going,' said Wes, as someone turned the stick between their palms until the skin was red and raw. That was me, I'm sure. 'Keep going. It's nearly there. It always catches in the end.'

We kept on sneaking glances though. None of us could look away.

'He's still there,' we whispered over our non-smoking sticks.

'He's still there,' we whispered, piling up our den with moss.

'He's still there,' we whispered as we climbed our tree.

'Leave it,' I said, or maybe it was Gabe, or Wes, or Bev. 'Not doing no harm to no one, is he?'

'What do you bloody care?'

'He's still there.'

So it's true that we were only playing. We were only playing when we shouted, 'Oi. What're you looking at?'

Leave it,' I said.

Or Wes said.

Or Bev said.

Leave the boy alone.'

'No,' Gabe said, and I know it was him that said it, not me. 'This is our river. You can't just sit there and stare. You have to pay the toll or move along. Why don't you go home?'

The boy didn't reply. He sat with his legs crossed like he was in assembly and the hymn was starting up. He sat with his back straight like we did when Mrs Pugh was doing the rounds with her ruler.

'Why are you here?'

'Maybe he doesn't speak English.'

'Perhaps he's deaf.'

'Throw something at him then. That'll stir him.'

Gabe picked up a stone from the bank and tossed it twice in his palm so it smacked in the middle and we all knew that it was a good one. He could have bowled for England if he'd wanted to. It was him that threw the stone.

He arced his arm above his head and hurled it with barely a grunt.

It wasn't the stone that did it though. No. It can't have been the stone that caused the blood because we saw the boy reach out a hand to catch it. We all saw it. He did it without flinching. Just reached up and caught the stone that Gabe had hurled with all his might. If it had cracked his head we would have applauded, but there was something horrible about the way the boy's hand flicked up and caught the stone mid-air.

'Did you see that?'

The boy put the stone inside his blazer pocket.

'Hey! That's our stone. Throw it back, why dontcha?'

He didn't though. He went on sitting and staring like nothing strange was happening to anyone.

The day got heavier. By that I mean the storm was closing in. You know how it gets. Your head feels tight. The air feels thick and everything is something like a dream. Even now when storms come up I get a migraine and I think about that day and everything becomes a blur of green and grey and red.

It was the kind of day that made you want to swim.

'Let him be,' said Wes, or Bev or me. 'Come on. I'm boiling up. Let's have a swim before our mams start calling us for tea.'

None of us had pants, so it was nudie dips or nothing for us all. We didn't think a thing of it back then and all of us were naked in the water, spinning round like baby seals.

It was Gabe who started with the splashing, I am sure of that. He got his arm an inch or so below the surface and he curved it through to send a wave of water up and over all of us. We joined in and, as we were the ones already wet, we started sending waves towards the boy.

Even then, when he was soaked right through, he didn't say a thing. He was soaking wet and had a stone inside his blazer pocket and he never said a word.

He stood up and Gabe laughed and pointed saying that the boy had wet his pants, but it didn't look like that at all. If anything it looked as though he'd vomited all down his front. His face was pale and grey and his eyes were suddenly red like he'd been crying, though if he had, we hadn't seen. He kept his shoes on as he slipped towards the river.

'Bloody hell! He's coming in.'

He kept his shorts on and his blazer and his hat and he let himself slide through the grass and right down to the river.

We were on him straight away.

He was clothed and we were naked. That was the thing.

We pulled at him. We had a sleeve. We took his hat. We pulled his shorts. We got his shoes. We span him up and ducked him underwater and we played him round and round and pulled his pants, navy little y-fronts that they were, until his peachy bum was bare.

There was splashing and shouting and screaming. But all of it was us.

He didn't fight back.

I don't know who first saw the stream of blood, but it was there and is always there between us now. This ribbon of red, like a string of leaves pouring down the middle of a river.

No one ever said a thing but we were out and grabbing at our clothes, all of us fighting with our shorts and our dresses and shirts, none of us looking at the water or each other. None of us speaking as we ran our different ways right through the woods and back to the estate.

We didn't meet again that summer back in 1962. Can you believe it was so long ago?

There was a rumour that a boy had died up in the woods, though my mammy said it was a lie. We'd counted all the heads and none of us was missing.

There was Gabe and Wes and Bev and me.

There was a stone that one of us threw across the river at a boy who caught it in his hand. There was a storm and a rope and a swing, and all of us, including the boy who smelled of sweets, all of us were only ever playing.

Alison Powell is a recent graduate of the MA in Creative Writing at Bath Spa University where she developed her novel *When the Mountain Swallowed the Morning,* a story set against the backdrop of the 1966 Aberfan disaster. She won runner-up prize in the 2015 Bridport First Novel Award, was long-listed for the 2016 Mslexia New Novelist competition and short-listed for the 2016 Janklow & Nesbit Bath Spa Award. Her short story 'Sparrow and Finch' featured in the December 2015 issue of *Mslexia* magazine. She is co-founder of the Bristol based WriteClub and also runs yoga and creativity retreats. www.alisonpowell.co.uk. Twitter: @alisonjpowell

The BSSA shortlist judges commented:

'We were intrigued by the unresolved mysteries in 'Who Said the River was Red?' and the shift between the narrator accepting responsibility and denying any real wrong doing. Did the children cause a boy to die all those years ago? The unusual questioning structure builds tension, as does the exact details of the escalating nature of the bullying. We end up being uncertain too, with many questions to ponder: the hallmark of a good short story.'

THE ACORN AWARD FOR AN UNPUBLISHED WRITER OF FICTION

NICK WERBER

Braces

Grandpa leans his round, radish pink face close, asks me to open wide and pushes a thick finger into my mouth. He yanks back my cheek like a fish on a hook and proceeds to prod at my teeth with a cold metal prong. Warm drool spills out of one corner of my mouth and cools on my cheek. Grandpa tilts the chair further back until my jaw falls open wide, slipping a tissue into my hand. As I wipe away the drool he reaches toward my back teeth, jabbing the prong into the molars.

There is a skeleton dangling in the corner. He has a metal rod sprouting out of his skull and his long arms hang loose by his sides. I try to lift my head up but the blood drains out of my skull and I feel woozy. I've been getting these dizzy spells lately. Mum says it is the hormones.

Next Grandpa takes a hook and begins scraping at my

incisors and I feel bits of tooth sloughing off until my mouth feels like the bottom of a kettle. Finally, the chair heaves forward.

'You have strong teeth,' Grandpa says, handing me a plastic cupful of purple liquid. 'A little crowded, but no fillings, yet.'

Outside the surgery is Grandpa's living room. Dad is lying on the couch watching the Grand Prix.

'You're looking a bit pale,' he says, as I pass in front of the television. 'Everything OK Pa?'

Grandpa hangs up his white coat in the corner and fixes his tie in the mirror, smoothing the remaining hair on his temples.

'We'll talk about it over lunch,' he says, moving toward the kitchen.

Dad turns the volume up on the Grand Prix and for a few minutes we watch the cars wind round the track, the engines gurgling in the Sunday silence. My eyes drift through the net curtains to the perfect green lawn that climbs upward toward Bognor beach, the sea beyond obscured by a vast rectangular hedge.

Bored, I get up and walk over to the large cabinets that run the length of one wall. Silver plates, boxes and some ornate candlesticks gleam behind glass. My favorite is a silver statue of a boxer with 'Israeli Boxing Championship 1951' etched on a plaque below.

'Was Grandpa a boxer?' I ask, but Dad is too mesmerized by the Grand Prix.

Grandpa appears in the hallway carrying a big plate of smoked salmon. He stops and glares at us until I tap Dad on the wrist and he jumps up, rubbing his hands together, mouthing, 'Lunchtime!'

In the dining room I lift a silver fork and feel the weight of it in my hand. We are crammed around the end of a long table, flanked by dark, old paintings on all sides.

'I learned a new word today,' I tell Grandpa. 'Somnambulist. It means a sleep walker.'

'Very good my boy,' he says. 'Words are good. But of course, science is better.'

'I like Science too,' I say.

'Nick's good at English,' Dad says. 'He writes stories.'

Dad tries to tell him about one of my stories, the one about the secret gate at the end of the garden.

'Stories are stories,' Grandpa says. 'It is time for him to think about having a profession.'

'Right, of course,' Dad says, his face looking like when he's been cut up at the lights.

'I like animals,' I say. 'I might want to be a vet one day.'

'Very good,' Grandpa nods.

'It's actually harder than being a doctor,' Dad says. 'And if he fails that, he can always, you know, be a dentist.'

Grandpa places his knife and fork carefully beside his plate and stands up, mopping his mouth with a napkin.

'Or he could be an out of work actor, like his father,' he says, turning toward the kitchen.

As Grandpa disappears, Dad grins at me across the table, signifying he has got one up on 'the old man' as he calls him.

When Grandpa emerges, he is gripping a big silver platter piled high with pink ham, cold beef and an assortment of salami, bread and coleslaw, that Dad would later describe as 'straight out of a packet.' Lumpy green gherkins lie like sea cucumbers around the edge.

Dad and I take two round slices of ham and a gherkin each. For a while there is just the sound of cutlery clacking onto plates and the cement mixer noises of Dad and Grandpa churning ham around in their mouths.

'The boy will need to have braces fitted,' Grandpa says gulping another mouthful of ham and rye bread.

I picture the night my older sister came home with her new braces and I wince slightly. Her face was red with tears and she went straight up to her room. Later I saw the brace floating in a glass beside her bed; a pink plastic shield bound by silvery, twisted metal. For months she shielded her smile, cupping a hand over her mouth. She told me her teeth ached.

'They look OK, don't they?' Dad says, squinting at me.

'If you want your son to grow up with crooked teeth, that is your decision,' Grandpa says, jabbing his knife toward Dad and then me. 'You want to have crooked teeth when you're older?'

I shake my head.

'How do you know they won't straighten out when he grows a bit?' says Dad.

'I know, because I know,' Grandpa says, his eyes fixing Dad.

'It's OK,' I say. 'I don't mind.'

I excuse myself from the table, and decide to spend some time outside. It is March and though the late afternoon sun appears at intervals through the clouds there is a cold wind that strays along the coast. I climb the lawn, listening to the hiss of the sea pulling back the shale. At the gate, I gaze back at the house, as an amber sun glows in the windows.

As soon as I am beyond the sight of the house I pull the cigarette and lighter I took from my dad's coat pocket and spark up. It's not my first one but I'm still getting used to it. My lips sting as I pull the smoke deep into my lungs, then I splutter as it puffs out. I do this for a few more times, until I feel a buzz, then I stub it out on a pebble to save for later. Along the beach I look for washed up and wind dried remains. I run a finger over a blistered bladder wrack, stiff and black, then pick up a shard of driftwood and throw it, just to see how far I can. On the bow of an old wooden boat, piled up on bricks, a seagull lands. It pads its webbed feet and picks at its white plumage with a hooked yellow beak. If Dad were here he would probably throw a tiny pebble in to the wind to see if the seagull flew up to catch it.

Down at the water's edge I try to skip stones but the surf is churning and each stone gets lost in a wave. I stare down the length of the beach as it curves into the distance. Millions and millions of pebbles mounting up to a long row of walls and perfect square hedges, and behind them, houses filled with people who never even go on the beach.

For a minute I think of them in their houses; watching snooker, or eating plates of hot roast chicken and beef and talking about the weather. Then I wonder how many people are standing on beaches around the world right now and how different they're all feeling. Maybe someone in Australia is standing barefoot on a white sand beach, as the sun comes up. Maybe they've got a surfboard in their hand and are about to dip into the warm water, paddle out to where the waves are building, ready to ride one back to shore.

And I'm in Bognor.

Dad likes our drives down here from London. Not because he is looking forward to seeing 'the old man', but because it gives us a chance to talk. He's always trying to get us to 'bond'. I don't mind the drive down though, and Dad has some good music. On the way here we listened to Abbey Road by the Beatles and the Joshua Tree by U2. Dad says it is good that we like the same music, as Grandpa always called anything he played 'nonsense'. Sometimes he says things out loud that he's thinking. Today he said, 'I love my Father, but that doesn't mean I have to like him.'

It's not the first time he's said it, either.

I wait around on the beach until the sun starts to go down and the wind gets even colder then head back up the slope, hands in pockets, churning the pebbles underfoot.

From the lawn, in the dark, I catch a glimpse of Dad and Grandpa though the window. I can tell they are having a 'serious' talk. Dad's leaning on his palm, creasing the skin around one eye. Grandpa knots his hands and frequently thrusts a finger at dad, like a pistol.

Grandpa has been trying for a while to get my dad to go back to working in his old job, the one he quit a year ago to be a full time actor.

I remember Dad told me once about a play he was in at school. Grandpa was in the audience and at the end Dad's housemaster went up to Grandpa and said he thought Dad had 'real talent'. He said Grandpa should think about sending Dad to drama school. Dad was really happy to find he was actually good at something, but Grandpa snubbed the housemaster and walked away without shaking his hand. The next year he moved Dad to a school that didn't even have a drama department. I suppose that's why Dad's always telling me, 'You have to go for your dreams'

At the door Grandpa gives me a vice like handshake, then uses the claw on my neck as he leads me out to the car where Dad is sitting, all ready to go. 'You are a good boy,' Grandpa says, squeezing my neck a little harder. 'Work hard now and you will have less problems later.' I force a smile through the neck pain and hug my arms around his big, firm stomach, until I hear the engine rev that says, 'Hurry up'.

In the car on the way home we are both silent. Dad wears driving glasses with yellow lenses that he thinks make him look cool. As the car pulls through the night I watch the orange street-light get sucked through the dark interior in waves, until I feel sick. Whenever I look across to Dad, he's got his concentrating face on.

'Do you like your school?' he says eventually, without looking at me.

'It's OK,' I reply.

'I mean, do you want to stay there, or would you mind going to another school?'

'Why?' I ask.

'You know money is tight, don't you?'

'I suppose.'

'Look if you want to stay, we'll find a way of paying. It's just...'

'Whatever, Dad.'

'It's not me,' Dad says, holding his hands up in a not guilty pose. 'You know what Grandpa is like with money. It comes with, conditions.'

'What's he asked for?'

Dad grips his fingers tighter on the wheel. 'He wants you to choose all sciences next year, and he'll only pay if you get A grades.'

'Really?' I say.

'You can always go to the comprehensive.'

'And lose all my friends?'

Dad pulls on to the motorway, slips across the lanes.

'I'll never get all A grades,' I say.

Dad sighs, 'Life's not easy, you know. THAT IS WHY YOU MUST HAVE A PROFESSION.' This last bit he says in a robot voice.

As the car drifts through the night, I start thinking about Grandpa's request and how fathers always seem to want to make their sons do what they want them to. Even Dad does it. He wants me to read books and be 'creative' like him. He doesn't force it down my throat like Grandpa does, but I'm kind of like a fish in his tank and he is making sure the water is the exact temperature he likes.

As we come to the 'halfway' roundabout, I slip my headphones over my ears and listen to the only tape Dad won't let me play out loud, because it's rap and because 'it's abrasive.'

Then I shut my eyes and picture that beach in Australia; The soft white sand between my toes, the sun rising before me, the salt in my hair. And as the blue surf rolls beneath my board, I see myself pushing out, beyond the building waves, out into the ocean beyond.

Nick Werber was born in south London and studied creative writing at the Open University. He spent some years working as a journalist and filmmaker in the Peruvian Amazon rainforest and now works as a freelance creative. Nick loves to travel and spends as much time as he can going to different countries and making documentary films. Among other creative ambitions Nick would like to write novels, travel writing and children's books.

The BSSA shortlist judges commented:

'This is a well-judged story about father/son relationships and the pressure to conform to family expectations or to go your own way. The further layer about the narrator being drawn into the conflict between his father and grandfather adds complexity, while vivid details and a strong sense of character and place combine to create a satisfying and rich read that appealed to us all.'

COMMENDED
BUNMI OGUNSIJI

Blessing

In the past she had made allowances for the Captain's absurd behaviour, the way he never answered her, nor did he ever look at her when she spoke to him, the cassava grain he offered without water, dry like that to her tongue. Quirks of old age, she had told herself. But the morning she had found him pouring Guinness over her bowl of Shredded Wheat and discovered crumbs of burnt, oily Akara in her underwear, Blessing concluded that a malevolent presence had taken up residence in her husband's mind and was slowly, mercilessly devouring the good sense and decency which had been the backbone of her husband's character. She had had to apologise on several occasions to a traumatised Pastor Jacob and an indignant congregation for the Captain's spectacular profanity in church. Where did he learn such words? And now, in the early hours of the morning, yams, three of them, floating like stools in the bath.

Blessing turned off the taps and bent slowly to pull the plug, letting out a raucous fart as she did so. It seemed to relieve her a little of the heavy discomfort in her heart, recalibrating her to a degree, this common and normal bodily occurrence alongside the absurd. *The Captain is lost at sea.* She had said this to Dr Qureishi but all he had wanted to do was throw tablets at her husband. *Haloperidol* this. *Risperidone* that. Foreign words. *This behaviour, though worrying is not uncommon,* Dr Qureishi had said. *This,* along with the restlessness which plagued her at night, *was to be expected,* the doctor had said. *A natural part of getting old.* What did he know about getting old? Him, not long out of nappies, with all the letters of the alphabet after his name and too many certificates on the wall and that ridiculous forest on his chin. Blessing had sat in the waiting room rubbing the Captain's cold and calloused hands, fingers hardened by life and DIY. She had watched through the opaque curtains of her failing eyesight, the video biographies of all the young doctors who worked in the Beech Tree surgery. But Blessing was not interested in Dr Qureishi's extra-curricular activities or his passion for rock climbing. Even the Devil can love baking bread and only the Devil would prescribe tablets designed to make a person forget where they are when all they want to do is be found.

The water drained, three yams, motionless in the bath, Blessing shook her head from side to side and caught her reflection in the bathroom mirror. Where was the girl from Mushin, Lagos, the one in the indigo dye dress, her with the soft curly afro and the gap between her two front teeth? Who was this grey haired, troubled woman fading through the years? She untied the belt of her dressing gown to relieve the stubborn gas in her belly and gathered the words of a prayer to Oluwa, God above. *What manner of nonsense is this? What manner of nonsense? What manner of nonsense?* It caught her then, the draught, alerting her to an opening somewhere in the house she had shared with the Captain for forty happy, settled years. She thought of her three solid boys, Ayo, Femi and Olu, all of them as wide as God's grace and as tall as the ladder you needed to get to him. If only they were here. *Over, under, now pull both ends and make a bow.* She had taught them all to tie their shoe laces and now her hands, shaking uncontrollably, suddenly confused and displaced, fumbled with the belt around her waist.

Into the dimly lit corridor... *What manner of nonsense,* the light left on like that and bills to pay? Her backless slippers sweeping the worn carpet beneath her feet, the strength of God in the marrow of her soul, propelling her forward, she tiptoed, so as not to disturb the beast surely lurking somewhere downstairs, tiptoed, carefully lifting and placing her feet on each step so as to avoid another fall.

She had a feeling she might find it like that, the front door wide open for anyone and everyone and Satan's family to enter. Blessing pushed the door shut, her gaze falling upon the phone on the hallway table, off the hook and beside the receiver the blue striped Avon bag she had used while selling lipstick and cold creams to the other sea wives in the boarding house, all of whom like her, waiting for the end of a voyage, a husband returning, a life promised. The bag was worn through at the corners, mysterious particles of dust seeping from the tiny holes. And again it came, the mantra she could not silence. *What manner of nonsense? What manner of nonsense? Benjamin?* She threw his name to the night in the hope that her husband would be handed back to her, a little cold perhaps, maybe worse for wear but... *home.* Nothing and no one returned. Blessing turned towards the light coming from underneath the living room door. *Benjamin, this is not a joke. What is wrong with you eh?* Again nothing. Time seemed to hold its breath as she played numerous scenarios in her mind, none ending well, and concluded that though elderly and disabled by age her spirit was a fighting one and she would not under any circumstances be afraid in her own home. She opened the cupboard under the stairs and took hold of the Captain's long beach umbrella. It had sheltered her from the storms that had come with their new life, it would protect her now. Blessing adjusted her grip, clutching the hand carved wooden handle with intent just as she had been taught to in the self-defence classes at Lambeth College she had attended before her fall. It was something to do. She could flick a stick, hold an umbrella or a walking cane like it was lethal. And she would do that now if need be. She crept towards the living room, nudged the door open with the end of the umbrella and switched on the light, her hand trembling as she held the makeshift weapon above her head ready to descend. But there was no intruder, only the Captain sitting upright in his favourite leather chair, one hand flicking the dust from the striped shoulder pads on his immaculate uniform, and the other stroking the wild-eyed fox perched as though he lived there, on her husband's lap. Blessing let out a high-pitched scream and threw her umbrella at the petrified creature bolting through her legs, into the darkness behind her. *Benjamin, why you let the devil in? Why you just there like that?* She could hardly catch her breath to admonish the Captain, her confusion growing moment by moment as did the black ink stain on the breast pocket of her husband's otherwise pristine uniform. *Why you wearing that Benjamin?* Suddenly the Captain was on his feet, legs slightly astride. He waved Blessing out of the way with a flick of his hand, an indecipherable grunt, and marched out of the room. *What manner of nonsense?* A fox in her home, three yams in the bath and her husband, despite the doctor's empty assurances, eternally lost at sea.

Daylight peeped over the trees as Blessing set out to retrieve the man she had married fifty years before, her eyes defiant under the blanket of night, though even with the street lamps she struggled to make out where the sky ended and the pavement

began. But she kept on, dust falling from the Avon bag leaving a trail behind her, the Captain's parka coat folded over her arm. Of course she would follow and not even they, the three young men skulking behind her would dampen her resolve.
Take what you want I'm not scared of you.
She emptied the contents of her Avon bag onto the pavement. The young men stared at the strange ash illuminated under night light, drizzling like angel dust, covering concrete.
We aint gonna trouble you.
I don't care what you going to do.
You shouldn't be out this late granny. You'll get lost.
Stop talking to me as though I am your family. I know where I am.
One, a lad more reticent than his friends, knelt to gather Blessing's things: old Avon magazines, dress making patterns from Woman's Own 1977, '78, '79 and five tattered National Savings books, their corners snipped off to remind the holder they were no longer valid. As he gathered her past in his hands stuffing it into the torn cotton lining the young man kept his eyes on Blessing then turned on his heels, catching up with his friends as they continued walking in the opposite direction. Boys to men. Gone.

She ignored the sidelong bemused stares of passengers on board the 133 and tutted loudly at the young woman with the blond beehive hairdo who came over to the driver's window to ask if she needed any help. *What manner of nonsense is this? People in this country…Ah!* She was simply asking the driver if her Freedom pass would take her all the way home and when he had asked her with his cigarette breath so strong it came through the plastic shield, where home might be, she had told him, Lagos.

It was almost impossible for her to negotiate the narrow steps leading to Queen Elizabeth Walk but God's strength was in her bones so she stood her ground, placing her feet just so and she walked, walked from there to Tower Bridge. From there to here and it was easy for her to spot the commanding figure dressed in white from head to foot, standing erect, his hands down by his side as if posing for a portrait picture. The Captain surveyed the coming and going of vessels along the River Thames, his stripes aglow in the sharp early morning sunlight.

You'll catch cold Benjamin.

The Captain continued to stare into the distance.

Benjamin.

Blessed tugged at the Captain's sleeve.

Benjamin?

The young man taking pictures of HMS Belfast turned to face her. At first irritated by the interruption then bemused by the sight of an elderly woman in her dressing gown and backless slippers, holding a coat she should surely have been wearing on such a cold morning.

Benjamin.

The young man shook his head.

Benjamin.

No sorry I'm not…Have you lost someone?

Blessing stared at him as if he were speaking a foreign language.

Can I call someone for you? Benjamin? Is that your son? Your husband?

Blessing glared at the young man and unzipped her Avon bag.

Don't be ridiculous. Benjamin is here.

She dipped her hand in, scooped out a handful of dust and held it up to the young man's face. *See? Here, let me help you put this on,* said the young man gently unfolding the parka, draping it around Blessing's shoulders.

I want to go now...I've left them…the children…in the bath.

Let's get you inside then, in the warm. We'll get you a cup of tea.

The young man tapped 999 on his mobile phone.

I need to go home

Do you know where that is? Do you know where home is?

Blessing looked out across the murky Thames, her gaze on a

time and place somewhere far in the distance. From Lagos to Liverpool to London…

There she whispered, *over there.*

Bunmi Ogunsiji is the Nigerian-British London-based writer, mother of a bright, sardonic teenager and (finally) a blogger – www.imguessingrehabdoesntcount.wordpress.com (based on absurd conversations with a certain bright, sardonic someone). A performance poet in a former lifetime, my script for children was shortlisted in the BBC Scriptroom competition 'Get A Squiggle On' and in 2016 (momentous for a number of reasons, including turning 50 with a smile and finally honouring my feet with a pair of comfortable shoes), I was delighted to have been longlisted for the Bath Flash Fiction Award and shortlisted in the Mslexia Women's Short Story Competition – a very good year so far...

Mair Bosworth commented:

'I was impressed by this story, which worked with themes seen in other stories – dementia, ageing, immigration – but in a fresh, surprising, effective way. Moving storytelling of great empathy and insight.'

COMMENDED
MARGARET DOLLEY

The Earth on the Way Down

The woman hangs in the display case, arms tucked round leathered knees. Irene fishes a crumpled tissue from her sleeve, and rubs at the fingerprints left by a blow-through of school children. The glass squeaks. The Early Iron Age is a side gallery of the museum, and the cleaners aren't as thorough as they used to be. She spits on her tissue, rubs harder. The whorls swirl and disappear.

Tell me, Irene says. The woman's eyelids, level with her own, are waxy blank half moons. She'd have been a beauty once, with her time-reddened hair and cheekbones sharp enough to slice through peat. Her cubed glass tomb rides on a solid beech wood plinth. If you hauled her up and out, and unbent her spare dry frame, she'd be a good foot shorter than a modern woman.

Tell me, Irene says. She'd have had a Nordic sort of name. Like Freya. Or Audhild. Tell me, Audhild, Irene says, and shakes her head. It's bad sign when you start talking to yourself. She returns to the straight-backed chair placed sentry-style across the room. Reaches in her handbag for the volume of the Eddas she found when clearing Colin's study. Volunteers may read, but today the smell of floor-polish is heavy on her head. She cannot keep her place.

Besides, she should stow her book the instant a visitor arrives. She should leap to her feet then and *engage*. Last month she helped remove the last of the leaflets explaining the bog burial from the cupboard within the plinth. It's all interactive now: she must *interpret* for the visitors.

Interpret what? The semicircle of amber beads, the remnants of a cowhide cape and the grains of barley and flaxseed extracted from Audhild's gut. The archaeologists can analyse last meals, but they can't agree on why she ended in the bog. Irene has read the evidence carefully. The teeth suggest late teens. Audhild was never pregnant; they can tell this from her pelvis. Irene's fingers flutter regretfully at her own.

'Penny for them, Mrs Underhill.' The supervisor has come up silently through the Bronze Age, the next-door room, avoiding any of the floorboards that are known to creak.

Irene startles, drops her book. 'I'm just … It's been so quiet.'

He taps on his watch, and thrusts it near, too near, her face. 'What does this say?'

'Ten-thirty.'

'Which means?'

'I don't need a break. I'm more than happy-'

'Think of the others. If you don't go for coffee, it sets a precedent. The paid staff get particularly annoyed. And then they're moaning in my office. Take twenty minutes. Now.'

Irene slips her arms into her beige angora cardigan, which has felted and lost its shape. She draws it round her chest: it would almost wrap round twice.

'Anyway, how many sessions have you done this week?'

Why should she tell him?

'Seven,' she says.

'And you're always stuck in here.' The volunteers are supposed to circulate throughout the entire museum. But Irene prefers this side gallery; she avoids the popular, noisy spots, like the Mummy or the Viking treasure trove.

'I like the Early Iron Age.' She makes her mouth smile and suppresses a wince as she bends to retrieve her bag. The gnawing in her colon has returned.

'It's good that someone likes it,' the supervisor says. 'The others find her creepy. When they're rostered alone here, they complain.'

At least he didn't say, haven't you got a home to go to, like he did last week. Irene's flat is well appointed, above a florist's shop. It was much the best they'd viewed, although Colin subsequently grumbled about the noise, the early-morning deliveries in the street below, why people had to shout so. At least it's not a chip shop, she'd told him, or a bar. The noise from that would have lasted half the night. They'd viewed the apartment on a bright day, but now it's crammed with their plump armchairs and mahogany bookcases chosen for a more gracious space, and she can't breathe.

In the cafeteria, a queue has formed. Jacinta is holding forth in its middle, and gesticulating at the clutch of volunteers by her side. Irene retracts her head between her shoulders, tortoise style, and hangs back, pretending to study the notices on the board.

Jacinta used to be a teacher – drama and religion – and wears swirly turquoise drapes and dangly earrings in a Grecian style. She's a natural museum guide, with a delivery that's light but loud, and a knack for choosing details that are perfect for the clients. Beside her, Irene feels even more beige. And yet Jacinta's nice: when they trained together as volunteers it was Jacinta who noticed Irene on the edge, and tried to draw her in.

Being on one's own offends, Irene thinks.

When it's safe to move, she shuffle-steps towards the till

with her eyes clamped firmly on the trays of cakes in plastic coats. Colin had loved her baking. She can leave the cupcakes, with their sickly icing, but there's also Battenberg oozing jam and a Bakewell with a flutter of almond on the top. She checks her purse, and settles for economy: a three-pack of custard creams.

She finds a quiet seat, takes out her bottle of Dicolin and blows upon her tea. Laughter drifts across from Jacinta's table. A couple of women who Irene remembers from a walking group catch sight of her. They almost bump brows as they bend to whisper together, and look guiltily away. Thank God that Colin had gone before the museum decided to take on unpaid volunteers. Irene stirs her tea, and resists the urge to dunk.

On her walk back through the galleries, back through time, she looks for spaces. It's the spaces between objects that hold interest for her now, not the artifacts themselves. Cupboards or alcoves into which one could snuggle and hide from sight: behind the rich drapes in *Victoriana*, under the four-poster in *Elizabethan World*, or beneath the bench in the pitch black audiovisual room where *Raiders from the North* is on permanent loop.

Safely back in the Early Iron Age, she retrieves her book of Eddas. The wise woman, the völva, is singing of Baldr and Hodr, in a new world, after the great destruction, where the earth is again sprouting abundance.

'How did she die, Miss?'

A group of schoolkids stand before her in a cloud of chewing gum. They wear washed out jade sweatshirts, and clutch the clipboards they were handed at reception.

'Is there a button to press?'

Irene rises from her chair and reminds herself: *engage*. 'You have to read the notice, dear.'

'The Mummy room had headphones. And an iPad thing.'

A dumpy girl with thick glasses and startled starfish eyes leans forward. 'Eye-ron age peat burial,' she reads. 'Miss, what's peat? Is it a name?'

'Well, there are different theories –' Irene opens her mouth to explain. No, to *interpret*.

'Her skin's all walnutty. And why's her hair so red?'

'The water in the bog dyed it, dear. Carbon dating shows-'

'This is boring, miss.'

A cocky looking boy bonks his classmate on her head.

'There isn't a question for this room you eejit. You should have checked the worksheet. Quick, we're losing time.'

And they're gone. Their voices stream away through the next gallery, through the time-greened shields and timeworn axe heads of the Bronze Age, and echo in the distance.

Irene looks across at Audhild, and from under mild podded eyelids Audhild looks back at her. The bog from which they dug her holds many secrets. Did she slip and fall during a ceremony to placate a god? Was she a wrongdoer, led there on a tumbrel and cast in? But there's no rope mark round her neck, no sign of blows upon her skull. The latest theory is that she was sacrificed.

Tell me, Irene says.

There's a loud cough from the doorway.

'Did you get my letter?' the museum director says.

Irene pretends to study her Eddas. The envelope she's using as a bookmark had summoned her for a meeting at two o'clock.

'Mrs Underhill, we need to talk.'

The director's not a bad man, just weak-chinned and a bit effete, with his gold cufflinks and fusty woollen waistcoat. With the same sheep eyes he had used when he glanced up from his desk last year and saw that Irene had come to volunteer. All the applicants had to fill out forms, tick boxes and have an informal chat.

'I just wonder that you don't mind …' he'd said. 'That it's not too soon.'

Irene snaps her book shut now.

'Talk about what?' she says.

'I know how much the museum means to you. Your

dedication …' his voice trails away. 'We love your commitment. But these are strictly part time slots.'

'I'm very happy with that. I don't need money.'

'Mrs Underhill, I've added up your hours. You're spending all week here. I've had the staff association in.'

'But no one else cares for the Iron Age.'

'That's not the point. The staff association says the scheme is getting out of hand. Volunteers are great. They bring a range of voices and have the gift of time: time to engage our clients that a regular employee can't spend.'

Spit it out, she wants to say.

And he does. 'So I've agreed to create two new half time paid posts. Jacinta, for example, but … how to put this … you need to take a break.'

Not whole days alone, whole days in the apartment stuffed with too many too big things from her old home. No space to breathe, or turn around. Just waiting, waiting.

Irene's voice, when it finally does come, is a half howl.

'A break?' She drops her bag and book and surges towards him and the director steps back nervously.

'It's not just you. We're saying the same to all the volunteers. And it doesn't have to be forever. A few months to begin with, and we'll review.'

'But what about the Iron Age …' Over his shoulder, in her display case bathed in light, Audhild watches and listens, perpetually suspended in her slit in time.

'Our consultant has had a good look at what he calls the visitor flow,' the director says. 'This gallery will be mothballed. The exhibits will go into deep storage in the basement. We'll throw our resources into a few key themes that will really sell: the Mummy, the Spitfire, the Tudor pageant boat.'

The artifacts with easy answers. He doesn't meet her eye.

'Did you hear me, Mrs Underhill?'

'Whatever you say. It'll give me more time for my … garden.'

'How long does the current rota last?' he asks.

'Until next Friday.'

'Right then. Let's make that your final shift.' He hesitates as he goes to leave the gallery, and uses her first name, the name he used to use, for the first time in over a year. 'Irene, I'd like us to have lunch then. Please.'

He names the good Italian across the road where she often came to lunch with Colin. The director had sat in the back row at the crematorium, and had run off at the end, just like today, with a limp shake of his hand.

She closes her eyes and shakes her head, shaking away the metallic odour of chemo, the arm-bruising drips, the rustle of plastic aprons and the indignity of cardboard kidney bowls. Nurses asking if there is anyone they can ring, suggesting volunteers who are trained to talk.

She crosses the gallery and stands with her hands pressed against Audhild's cubed glass tomb, staring at her leathered flesh folds and calm face.

Audhild would not have left alone. There would have been a crowd calling around her beneath the forge-grey northern skies, ravens cawing overhead, the tide slumping in the distance.

Was she scared when they led her out, or did she go willingly? Was she still sentient when she landed in the bog? Did she panic as its viscous brownness sucked her down? Did she open her mouth to scream, taste peat upon her tongue and twist and choke? And gag on soil, inhaling damp dark earth? Did she corkscrew and try to fight her way back upwards, back to life? Or did she tumble into acquiescence, with a premonition that immortality waited in her later afterlife?

Irene bends and slips open the door beneath the glass. The cupboard in the plinth has room enough for one. She lays her handbag at the far end, and smoothes her cardigan around it. Yes, a pillow. If she curls up foetus style, there is ample space. There. Just so. She splays her fingers against the inside of the door and slides it gently shut. Her breathing settles in the dark. The Diconal fizz insistence on her tongue.

Margaret Dolley grew up in Belfast and spent a lot of time in the mummy gallery in the Ulster Museum – which may have helped to inspire her story for this competition. She studied Swahili at university and lived in Tanzania, New Zealand and in London before moving to Luxembourg, where she now works as an editor. She began writing short stories in her head doing laps in her local pool, as part of a yet-to-be-realized attempt to swim the English Channel. She is currently putting the finishing touches to a novel, set on an imaginary island off the west coast of Ireland

Mair Bosworth commented:

'A great beginning and an even better ending in this story of a museum volunteer's fascination with the Iron Age bog body under her care. I loved how this story placed something very strange and dark against something apparently mundane. It unsettled me and stayed with me long after reading.'

COMMENDED

KATHY STEVENS

A Marriage of Convenience

He's a handsome boy, Aalimah's husband.

Sometimes she just watches him, like you might watch a pleasant view – a slow sunset, or a thunderstorm – for the sheer, constant individuality of him. She watches him in the knowledge that no one will ever see him exactly as she sees him in that one, small moment; the angle of an eyebrow, and the fine veins in his eyes from a heavy night on the wine, which, somehow, only make him lovelier. The strands of tar-black hair always fall differently, and he blows them away from his face with faux impatience, like his beauty is nothing more than a small annoyance to him, a mosquito. He knows she watches him but pretends he doesn't catch her, a small curve of the upper lip the only indication that he isn't oblivious to the admiration his physical appearance has always demanded. He is more than used to it. He's sharp and square shouldered, clipped and neat. Skin the texture of a downy peach and the colour of dark rum, or treacle. He smells of orange blossom, cumin, coriander. Baadir is a chef, but even when he isn't working he smells the same, even after a shower. When they were first married she hid his aftershave to see what he'd smell like without it, but he was just the same to her. He laughed when she told him what she'd done. She always tells him what she's done, *I went to... I kissed a... I think I love...*, and more often than not, he laughs. He is shorter than her, so when she takes him to work parties she must wear flat shoes, which are not flattering to her ankles. He says her ankles are not flattering to the shoes and she taps him on the back of his glossy head, calls him *Short Arse* while he calls her *Lanky Bitch*, which never ceases to amuse them both. They do not talk like this in front of their respective parents, although she does tap his head, occasionally, in front of her mother. In her mother's eyes, his height is his only flaw. Aalimah, for once, agrees.

He's leaving for work now, and he kisses her, taking time over the gesture. It is important to them both, this ritual. She submits to his embrace, limp as McDonald's lettuce. He leaves a warm dab of moisture on her cheek that she does not brush away, even after he's gone, letting her skin dry naturally. His invisible mark is as real to her as a wax seal on a love letter; it's a stamp that certifies their union, if not before God then between themselves. There are, after all, four people in their marriage, and God isn't one of them. Aalimah has privately issued the numbers: Baadir is one (of course) and she is three (logically). She supposes if God was to have a number he'd be somewhere around thirteen. *Unlucky for some,* she says to the burgundy kettle they chose together. She fills the void he has made by making a cup of very sweet, milky tea – cinnamon, star anise, ginger – and leaves her seat at the dining table, which is spread with crisp sheets of A4, to perch at the breakfast counter.

She sips short and quick, as she often does when she thinks

about God, and flips her wallet open, snaps it shut. She does this several times, *flip and snap*. The sun is beginning to break through the dawn, and she squints in the light of a new day. Her feet are cold, but her face is hot and her forehead perspires. She fans herself with her wallet, which is made of sturdy brown leather and contains only a few things; she does not believe in debris, in the dregs of life that people are wont to carry around. There are only: two bank cards, a driver's licence, a library card and a single slip of paper – a cutting from a newspaper. She removes the cutting now, reads it without seeing the words. She has carried it so long that the paper is fluffy and soft, like the inside of a puppy's ear. The edges are an ugly, soiled black, from the dye of her wallet and the grease in her hands. From its own bleeding print. She has read it so often that the words have lost their meaning; it is her rabbit's foot, this newspaper cutting, and she would feel unprotected without it, like a character in a corny 90's video game, facing an endboss without a pixelated amulet. She realises, quite suddenly, that she is holding it and she drops it on the counter as if it's hot. Takes up her tea once more, which is tepid by comparison.

Around her, practical things sit on expensive surfaces. An angle poise lamp, ugly enamel white, squats on the statement dining table they only ever use one corner of at a time. Her dainty soldering iron is poised and ready for use on the other end to her scattered papers; there are delicate pieces of filigree silver surrounding it in various stages of completion, and small burn marks, scalded deep into the wood. Her foot is banging on the leg of her stool, knocking out a rhythm – she always turns to the music in her head when she is waiting – the foot is getting numb but she doesn't notice. Even if she did notice she wouldn't stop. There is no television in this or any room of the house, instead there are books left in piles where a television might be. Aalimah and her husband select books each evening from these piles as though selecting a TV channel, and drape themselves over the furniture to read, their warm, brown limbs hung artfully over the arms of chairs, fingers and toes skimming the hardwood floor, and lips moving silently as though they're having a secret conversation. They read each other's recommendations but never discuss them. The first time they met (darkness broken by neon flashes, red wine for him and cappuccino for her, shoes sticking to the dirty floor, someone else's chip by her elbow) she'd said: *the intimacy of shared reading can be so easily broken by the brashness of opinion,* and whether he agreed or not, he has never divulged. She loves him for this. She loves him for so many things.

They once took a drunken personality test online, which proclaimed him to be a Hedonist and her a High Achiever. They argued with the screen, flecks of rainbow moisture hitting and sticking there, slim, healthy arms across bare shoulders and tears of uncomplicated joy rolling down their cheeks. In retrospect, the personality test was right. Frightening how a Facebook quiz knows her better than her mother. *Uneducated flesh and passionless blood,* she says aloud in the empty room. Baadir is undoubtedly a hedonist. She looks across the room where his violin hangs from the wall by the dining table. It is only one below a Stradivarius, but he plays it every day and the neck is slick from use. Little scratches around the F holes where his fingernails have grazed in the passion of his playing. He once told her solemnly that he was evicted from a flat when he spent three month's rent money on the instrument. She loves to look at it when she is thinking and when she's not. She loves to watch him play it - the rosewood sets off the fire in his skin and the music makes his eyes dance with more life than a thousand men. Baadir plays violin like her father plays golf, but his prowess is lost on her parents. She doesn't care; she prefers that he plays just for her. She is capable of jealousy.

More sugar, says Aalimah to herself. The heat of her tea had hidden its blandness, and now with cooling she can tell it is not like her mother's. Where Baadir is warm, almost hot to the touch and to the eye, Aalimah's mother is cool. A room seems to physically drop in temperature when her mother enters it - *maybe that's why she makes so much tea*. She makes the best sweet tea Aalimah has ever tasted, and Aalimah has tasted a lot of tea, all over England and Europe and China and India. Aalimah loves her mother but does not really like her. When she visits home, and holds her mother to her chest, she never sighs in that contented way a person should sigh when they know they have come home, there is no sense of relief. There are very few senses at all. In their place is an abundance of other things: calculation, planning, execution, as precise as Baadir's music and as cool as her mother's breath. Her mother embraces Baadir with more warmth than she can muster for her own daughter – she can see the relief in that particular embrace - and both her parents adore Baadir, though her father wishes he would take up golf, *It is a pastime for men*, her father tells her through his teeth when she has kept them at the first hole for more than five minutes. She only plays for the thrill of hitting something with a stick, *It is called a club*, her father likes to correct her. She also plays for the comfort of her father's limited conversation, his staccato words and awkward sentences that are so familiar. She enjoys the comfort of knowing a person completely who will never know the completeness of herself.

When she thinks of her family, her face stretches into an automatic smile which may be mistaken for happiness. In reality, it is something more and less and altogether complex – a mosaic of imbedded tradition and assumed love, the shards of a difficult conscience, struck together over time to form a firm sediment of half-formed opinions. She smiles her automatic smile now, stirring her cooling tea with a long naked fingernail. The tea is too sweet to drink, she has over-compensated. She sucks it from her finger, slipping her tongue beneath her nail, and still watching the violin. Her fingers rub at the slip of paper without her brain's knowledge or permission. They move with the quickness of habit.

A knock on their thick oak door comes to her now over the noise of her memories, echoing through the house. It's the beat of a song in her heart and she knows this particular rhythm well – *Dum, de-dum, dum dum*. She taps out a canon of the knock on her mug of chai and a new smile settles on top of the last one. She gets up to answer the door.

The room is empty without her, but for the practical things on expensive surfaces. The sound of Aalimah and her guest in the hall is muffled and secretive, as though they are ashamed. The sharp suck of an affected kiss of greeting in the air, some whispering, shoes being removed and falling with a clunk to the bare wood floor. A musical laugh that rings out very clear and sweet as a violin solo. And more kissing, soft and genuine this time, altogether different.

On the counter, the slip of paper lies beside a cold cup of tea and a good leather wallet. There is a teaspoon making a dent in a pool of cold milk, and the pool is slowly spreading as if it's alive, inching ever closer to the paper. The print is faded with the oil of Aalimah's hand – there is more ink in Aalimah than on the paper, now. It says:
Gay Muslim woman seeks similar man for marriage of convenience.
Must be professional, must be non-smoker.
Musician preferred.

The milk makes contact with the paper and the words begin to disappear in the dark spread of liquid. Above, two women are making love in the late morning, in a bed that smells of orange blossom, cumin and coriander. She'll make dinner later, for numbers one, two and four, but she isn't thinking of what she must buy, or about the table cloth that needs airing. She's forgotten the dullness of paperwork and the tiny pieces of silver. There is a quiet sigh in the air that seems to come from the house itself. The tea is cold now. The words on the paper are illegible.

Kathy Stevens first decided to try her hand at writing fiction when she was sacked from a terrible job in the summer of 2014; she'd always assumed she wasn't clever enough to write something people would want to read, but suddenly had the time to try. Since then, she's won Ad Hoc Fiction, Faber Academy QuickFic, been shortlisted in the Bath Flash Fiction Award, been published in magazines including *Prole* and *The Cadaverine*, been accepted to study a Creative Writing Masters at UEA, and had a serious increase in self-confidence. She has a BA (Hons) English Literature from Bath Spa University.

Mair Bosworth commented:

'I could see everything in this story, so clearly. And perhaps even smell it too! Which is all credit to the author's powers of description. I liked the slow reveal of the nature of this marriage of convenience and the warmth between the central characters.'

FFLUR DAFYDD

The Azalea Tree

His name was a gulp of gold. *Eurfyl.* The kind of name that singled him out for stickiness; for a lifetime of bedding down with bees.

The bees only came for me; never him. With or without the suit he claimed they would never touch him, that they respected him. 'They know me,' Eurfyl would say. 'They sting you, Lydia, because they can sense your fear, they can smell it — it's your sweat — it's like glue to them. But with me it's different. There's honey in my veins.' The implication being, of course, that there isn't a drop of honey in my veins; that I am simply resigned to pumping common, dark blood around my body — something that can't be potted up and made to glisten.

He told me all this while I was removing yet another stinger from my finger. He glared back at me from behind the veil of his beekeeping suit, his eyes like those of his bees; compound eyes, multiplying in their sockets, looking at everything and nothing all at once. I watched him go through the open doors, taking bold white strides across the lawn. Once, I would have found his gait graceful, beautiful even, but he looked ridiculous to me now, like some sort of colourless clown, flailing his arms around in the air. That's when I knew — that there wasn't an ounce of nectar left in me. That I was done with honey, and done with Eurfyl, and that the azalea tree was my only way out.

The keys of the delivery van glittered on the kitchen table. A little hint, more often than not, that I should be doing something to help him, now that I'd given up on working with the bees. Little did he know how much I enjoyed that sudden bolt from him in the delivery van. It always surprised me how comforting everything in the town appeared; the pale cottages like the faces of old friends, while the honey farm, shrinking from view in the rear view mirror, seemed like a stranger.

I used to stare up at the honey farm every night while I was wiping tables at the pub, thinking how much better it would be to live up there, to survey everyone from that great height. Eurfyl was a stranger to me then, simply the 'honey man' who used to sit and brood in the corner of the pub, nursing his mead. Always mead, never beer; only what the bees had intended for him. 'Too old for you,' the landlady said. 'Old enough to be your father. Or your grandfather, I should think.'

Everything looked so much better from the honey farm. The town, a pretty miniature, the lavender sea curling around it — it didn't seem like the dead-end seaside town I knew, where it only took you three minutes to walk from one end of the beach to the other. 'Stay,' he insisted, his sticky fingers snaking their way under my dress, 'just stay. Stay as long as you like. Move in if you want.' He didn't have to ask twice. I remember thinking that if I couldn't get out of the town, then climbing higher up into it was surely the next best thing. It was too dark, that night, of course, for me to be able to make out that silvery silhouette at the foot of the garden. I thought maybe it was a Wendy House, a *t -bach-twt*. I assumed he must already have kids, at his age. That he wanted something different from me. But if I'd have been closer I would have heard the din inside, the fizzle of a hundred tiny wings, and would have known that it was no play-house.

Vernon and Bet were already outside the shop, eagerly anticipating my arrival. Not so much for the blueberries-in-honey or the blackberry mead they'd ordered, but rather for the ooze of gossip, the latest instalment in the barmaid-and-beekeeper saga. It was best to stay put in the van.

'Eurfyl says there's no such thing as a blind spot,' I said, as I pretended to adjust the wing mirrors. 'He says if you lean out far enough, you should be able to see everything. Vernon, you don't mind getting the stuff out do you? I'm in a bit of a rush so...'

Vernon nodded. Beneath the clunk and clack of honey jars I could hear him mumbling something to his wife. I caught sight of Bet in the mirror, standing a little aslant, peering in at me.

'He's right, of course,' I heard Vernon say, as he walked back into the shop. 'Women drivers blame everything on blind spots.'

I had forgotten about the blind spot that is Bet Daniels. She came at me from the other side, poking her head in through the open window.

'Oh good God Lydia,' she said, her eyes resting on my stomach. 'I knew it. How far gone are you?'

'Eight months,' I replied quietly. Eurfyl joked that the flutters felt like the beating of wings, that really I was carrying a giant bee. Which wouldn't be surprising, the amount of mead he made me drink. It was only afterwards that I understood how mead was meant to bring forth a son, a little drone, an heir to the honey empire.

But of course it hadn't worked. If he'd been at the scan he'd know that.

'So I suppose that's it now then,' said Bet. 'It's not just a bit of fun anymore then Lydia. Not one of your whims after all.'

I could only imagine what she would say to everyone. That my attempts at climbing above them all had failed. That although I had gone up in my little world that I would be forced back down again; that this baby was going to make sure I was stuck to the town like never before, glued to it. That's what honey does, she once told me. It sticks to everything. Ever tried getting it off your hands? Even when it's gone it feels as if it's still there.

When I got back Eurfyl was in the shower. Lathering himself up in unperfumed nothingness from a big white bottle, too afraid to let any fragrance settle on him, for fear of enraging the bees. But the lack of colour and scent has always stifled me, making me long for the miniatures of perfume my mother used to keep; the glint of rose and amber and emerald, the little clouds of patchouli, geranium, and lavender.

'Dyw bywyd ddim yn fêl i gyd,' my mam always said, an old proverb in her mother tongue. 'Life isn't all honey.'

That was even before there was any honey in our lives.

The next morning he found me hunched by the azalea tree.

'Not still tending on that are you Lydia? I don't see there's much point, when the bees don't even care for it.'

Eurfyl has always insisted that his bees wouldn't go within a mile of an azalea tree. That its pollen is toxic to humans, that a batch of honey could be destroyed by it.

'It makes mad honey,' he said. 'There's no telling what the effects could be. It might even kill you.'

Far off in the distance I could see them, the worker bees, the females, whizzing back and forth. The drones, those arrogant males, were far away somewhere in the hive, just sitting there, waiting. Pottering around until they saw their chance to fertilise a queen bee. You would think they could find something useful to do in the meantime, like clean up the hive, but no. Day after day the worker bees return to the hive to find it a complete tip, honeycomb scattered like dirty clothing all over the place, and those lazy winged so-and-sos just look and shrug. Because they've only got one thing on their minds.

The drones are the victims of their own success. If they fertilise that queen bee good and proper, it's all over for them. Their days are numbered.

At that moment, the worker bees were right above me; a gathering of tiny wings. My sweat, that strange nectar, now ripe with life, had enticed them again. I lay there, arms laid out by my side. Eurfyl was right; once they knew you weren't afraid of them, they had no desire to sting. But they were still curious about the smell of my sweat, this strange pulsing inside me. It drew them closer and closer. As if the tree and I were one thing, as though my arms and legs were its branches. And then right at the last moment, they lost interest in me, and slid in under the pink canopies of the azalea tree.

By the time we were ready to gather the honey, I was too big to lean over by the beehive, or to be on my hands and knees in the garden. I told Eurfyl I'd stay inside to rest. 'Nonsense, it won't do you any harm,' he said, hoisting the starchy fabric about my bulging stomach, zipping me in. I caught sight of myself in the patio doors; a lumpy, inelegant mass waddling across the lawn. A bee-widow, dressed for some terrible tragedy.

I waited while he blew the bees out of the hive. I saw for a moment what I had seen in him in that pub more than a year ago. A dedication; a passion. But all too soon he was loading the heavy honey supers in my arms and ordering me back into the house and the last shred of affection had buzzed away, just like the honey bees.

I felt his presence behind me as I scraped the honeycomb off the frames. He paused in the doorway. I knew what he was looking at. The colour of the honey. I'd never seen a batch quite like it. A rosy elixir that flowed soundlessly into the bucket. Azalea blood.

'It really is a curious colour,' Eurfyl said, dipping a small spoon into it. He raised it to his lips, and paused. Inside me, our daughter topsy-turvied; a little worker bee, sloshing in the warm nectar.

'Taste it, Eurfyl,' I said, pressing the spoon against his mouth.

He took a spoonful. Then another. Then another. Finally, he looked at me. Almost through me. His irises seemed to take off, to fly away. At the corner of his mouth was the beginning of an odd, gloopy smile. In the distance I could hear the sea crashing, and the town holding its breath. As he fell to his knees, the spoon tilted and it seemed that my whole world tilted with it, dangling from that copper thread of hope in the air.

'Azalea honey, isn't it?' he said, looking up at me. He was trembling. 'They've turned against me again, haven't they? It's fine Lydia. Don't look at me like that. I'll be OK. I've had it before. I've had all the bad honeys – just in case. Just to know if I can handle them. I'm strong enough. It'll pass. It always passes.' He got up and fell down again, pulling me down with him. I tried to get up. But I couldn't. Bet was right. The honey had glued me to the spot.

'This feeling, this delirium,' Eurfyl continued, breathlessly, 'it's awful and wonderful at the same time. You should try some of that honey Lydia. Go on! Get up and dance with me, dance,' he said, grappling with my suit, pulling us both to our unsteady feet. 'Let's celebrate. Celebrate that we're going to have a son. He'll be with us soon. Any day now.'

I looked up as he spun me around. Even a drone would have been a comfort now. But the sky was empty. At the far end of the garden, the azalea tree had its pink head bowed, as though it couldn't meet my gaze. It had never been my ally. Like everything else, it was on his side. We no longer seemed like one thing. We stood separate and alone. And in the breeze the azalea tree seemed to dance with Eurfyl, to tremble and sway and mock just like he did, while in the distance the town that had seemed so small swelled suddenly like the sea, rising up over the cliff face to laugh at me.

Fflur Dafydd is a bilingual Welsh/English fiction writer, screenwriter and singer-songwriter. She recently wrote and co-produced a film adaptation of her Welsh-language novel *Y Llyfrgell* (The Library Suicides) which premiered at the Edinburgh International Film Festival, where it was nominated for Best British Feature. She has an MA in Creative Writing from UEA, and a PhD on the work of the poet R.S. Thomas. She considers the short story to be her 'first love' and, following the publication of her Welsh-language collection, *Awr y Locustiaid* (Hour of the Locust) in 2010, she is now working on her first collection in English.

THOMAS ATKINSON

Dancing Turtle

Mom took me to the Appalachian Festival today, which was almost to Cincinnati, along the river. Dad stayed home to move the bars up in the bathroom. We dropped down and took Route 32 – 'The James A. Rhodes Appalachian Highway' – for the better part of two hours. And when we passed the sign for Burnt Cabin Road, Mom said, like she always does, 'There's a story there.' She pointed out stands of corn, and fall-down barns, and every so often she'd turn and say, 'Molly, need to stop?' And I said, 'No.' Or at least the sound I make that we all know means 'no.' Like a wheel bearing going bad Dad says, if a wheel bearing going bad started with an 'n.' Holding my bladder has become something of a point of pride for me these last three years since, due to some difficulties during my birth, potty training ended and menstruation began in the very same month.

We parked up front in a blue sign space, and then we argued back and forth about my stupid rollator. It's a walker with wheels and a little seat with a wire basket underneath and bicycle brakes that I can't use very well anyway. I'd rather just walk my walk. An Indian doctor at Children's – an India Indian, not an American Indian – he told my dad it might help and that's all it took. Twelve hours of price shopping on the internet later, I was the not-so-proud owner of a shiny blue Medline Rollator with eight inch wheels to give me 'confidence on all terrains.' At least it wasn't the pink 'Breast Cancer Awareness' model. I think he was expecting more.

I finally got out, 'Geezers and fat ladies.'

She leaned on my door and smiled. She said, 'Are you sure? I told you, there's going to be a lot of walking.' Then she shrugged her shoulders and leaned in to help me out. She slipped her arms around me, her face warm in my neck, waiting for the touch of my twisted hands against her back. It's a dance we've done a million times, and the only graceful moment of my day, and sometimes, in that brief stillness before she says, 'Ready?' I pretend she's a boy.

It never happens with my dad because he still makes a fart noise against my neck like he did when I was little, then I act like I'm mad and he acts like he believes me. Mom fussed in her carry-all for a minute, and then, pretending like she'd just thought of it, said, 'I might bring it just for me. I can hang my bag on the handle and that little basket can carry all the crap your father's rightly worried we're going to buy.'

I hate that little basket.

There were men dressed up like pioneers with tall boots and string-laced shirts, and women with loose skirts and bonnets. And there were Indians, more than I'd ever seen in one place. Some were in costumes and feathers and war paint, but most were in their everyday clothes. There was a boy, not much older than me, in new jeans and a red western shirt with pearl buttons. His hair was long and black and he wore a heavy necklace white as bone. I tried to smile at him and I think he nodded in my direction.

There's Indians out our way too, the United Remnant Band of the Shawnee Nation. They're supposed to be what's left of the Shawnee that wouldn't move out west when Tecumseh died and, after all this time, a lot of them don't look much like Indians. They run a little cavern and Dad took me last spring. It was hard to get around and I didn't really like it inside there, eight inch wheels or not, so we walked around the pioneer village mostly. In the little museum, he stared at a stuffed buffalo head on the wall for a long time, and then turned to me and said, 'Guess it beats the other end sticking out of the wall.' He hunts, but I don't think he'd put any heads on our wall even if Mom let him. He hunts deer and wild turkey mostly. He used to hunt squirrel and rabbit too, until he brought home a rabbit once and I cried and cried. The deer and turkeys are all dressed-out and wrapped up in white butcher's paper by the time I see them, and once I tried venison breakfast sausage I won't eat anything else. In the gift shop, I wanted a tomahawk with a heart cut out of the black blade, but Dad just smiled and bought me a little leather side bag. He picked out some dreamcatcher earrings for Mom and I shook my head and managed to get out, 'She'll hate those!' It didn't sound like, 'She'll hate those!' but he understands. Then he smiled and said, 'Let's see.' The heavy woman behind the counter gave him that sympathetic smile, the one I always thought they should wait and give when I'm not in the room, or at least not looking right at them. Dad doesn't deal with my public very well. After he counted his change and we were working our way slowly out, he motioned with his head and said, in a loud voice, 'Indian Princess Eats Many Fry Bread.'

Mom hates those earrings, and whenever we need a laugh, he makes her to put them on. I keep the side bag by my bedside. There's four white shells from our trip to my uncle's in Florida, a Blue Jay feather and some eight-sided salt crystals big as dice, and a brass shell casing from when they shot off seven rifles at my grandfather's funeral.

When Mom and I passed another group of Indian women, I tugged at one ear and said, 'Your earrings?' It took her a minute to work out the sounds, but then she smiled.

We watched a blacksmith and listened to a bluegrass band. There was an old man with a long gray beard who made rocking chairs all by hand and a woman with bad teeth weaving round baskets she said were from Scotland. We watched two little black girls in matching dresses dip string in warm beeswax to make candles. Sometimes my mind gets caught, like watching that blacksmith blow those orange coals almost white, or watching those candles get bigger without ever seeing them get bigger, or that old man stripping bark with a drawknife. Then my mom or dad has to break my line of sight, just for a second, and when she got in between me and those candles, she said, 'Do you smell kettle corn?'

My mom is crazy about kettle corn. And judging from the line so is everyone else in Ohio, Kentucky and West Virginia. It ran the length of the walkway, blocking access to the fresh-squeezed lemonade, homemade fudge, wild game jerky and even the funnel cakes. And as we walked against the tide, getting eyed by everyone in line, like I might be faking to cut in, we could see the man working a big wooden paddle. He was stirring popcorn in hot oil in a three foot copper bowl, and a girl, maybe his daughter, was laying on the salt and sugar. When it was done, he grabbed a twisted wire handle on one side like the one on our wood stove, and flipped the whole batch onto a big metal table. The daughter and another girl were scooping, filling long plastic sleeves full of hot popcorn.

Mom said, 'What do you think? Half a bag or full? Can we eat a bag of kettle corn as long as your leg?' She sniffed the air for a moment, then said, 'Seems a shame to come all this way for half a bag. We can always take a little home to your father.' She looked around and said, 'Let's find you a place to sit.'

We found me a nice spot under a Sugar Maple, not too close to the families picnicking with small children, on the edge of a big field with a little tent in the center. She parked the rollator on the other side of the trunk, then she shielded her eyes from the sun to scan the long line again. She said, 'If I'm not back by sundown, start crawling for the car.' 'All akimbo' is how I would describe me sitting on the ground. As a matter of fact, it's probably how I would describe me. I love that word, 'akimbo.' I love the sound it coming out of someone else's mouth. Once he found out, my dad uses it all the time, usually joking that 'a kimbo' is a Japanese knife they sell on the Home Shopping Channel.

I got caught by a little ribbon of red cellophane, probably from a cigarette pack, waving in the gentle breeze like a tiny banner on a flagpole of grass. The PA system crackled an announcement but I wasn't paying attention. When the drumming started, I could feel it, feel it in the ground, right up through my seat. Indian drums. And even though I could see them banging on stretched hides, gathered around that little tent, the vibrations seemed to be coming from far, far away. Then the boy in the pearl button shirt stepped out from the tent with a microphone. He closed his eyes, the tendons of his neck tight against that bone necklace, and began chanting a song that seemed to have no words, just vowels and repeated syllables, droning low notes that were achingly familiar.

Two women in deerskin dresses began a slow shuffling dance in a wide circle around him. Other Indians fell in behind them and as they stagger-stepped around that field, they motioned for everyone to join them. Mostly it was little kids that did, little blond boys and girls looking for any excuse to run around. But there was something about that dance, the awkward hesitant rhythm of it, that reached right inside me. I called to those two women, and for the first time in my life, I knew it didn't matter if it sounded like the honking of a goose on the wing. I fell over on my side trying to get up, because I knew, I knew that I had to be out there. I rolled on to my stomach to push myself up, and as I battled my unforgiving body, two worn and beaded moccasins appeared at each elbow. They lifted me up, cooing comfort, the deerskin soft as velvet against my arms. We worked our way into the slow current of dancers, floating down like autumn leaves into that song. And when they finally let go, I was out in front, and everyone behind followed my skewed path, heads down and halting steps, to somewhere I've never been.

I don't know how long his song went on, or how many times I passed close by the boy in the bone necklace, close enough it seemed to me, to feel the breath of it on my cheek. I only know that I lived another life, that for the length of it the pain was gone, gone like it had never been, gone like the lost ghost of a memory. And when it was over, I shuffled in place before him, my eyes, fixed in the erratic orbit of my head, locked on to his. I said, 'I can hear your heart.'

He smiled, and then cocked his head to look past my ear, searching for my keeper.

I tried to sing it, still dancing at his feet, knowing the words were lost, knowing all he could hear was the awful music of my voice, like some small thing, caught in the fine wire of a snare.

Thomas M. Atkinson is an American author and playwright. His story 'Grimace in the Burnt Black Hill' will appear in *New Stories from the Midwest 2015*, and received two 2013 Pushcart Prize nominations. 'Me & Mr.Tinkles' will appear in the *Fish Anthology 2016*. *Standing Deadwood: Collected Stories* was a finalist in the 2014 Spokane Prize for Short Fiction and a finalist in the 2014 St. Lawrence Book Award for Fiction, and his new novel *TIKI MAN* was a finalist in the 2014 Leapfrog Press Fiction Contest. He has received five Ohio Arts Council Individual Excellence Awards.

INGRID JENDRZEJEWSKI

We Were Curious About Boys

We grew up in cornfields, our sun-kissed skin stretched tight over bone. We were all knees and elbows and longing, and we were curious about boys.

Oh sure, some of us had brothers, but from the time they were old enough to reach up and prize husked ears from stalks, they were called men, not boys. And by the time our brothers were as old as us, they were working the land, not sitting at desks. So it was only at school that we saw them: boys, real boys, boys with pale, smooth hands who played sport after school, played in the marching band, played, it was rumoured, with themselves.

Our men didn't talk much, worked hard, kept their tractors clean. The boys at school, they had clean clothes, clean fingernails, but their minds were dirty. We never spoke to them, of course, but there were things we thought we knew. Of course we were curious.

We thought about boys as we rose before the dawn chorus to milk cows, collect eggs, tend horses. We thought about boys as we tried not to fall asleep darning socks, mending potato sacks, rubbing vinegar on our already-calloused feet. We thought about them, how they went to bed early, woke up late. How they crowed like turkeys, puffed themselves up at school. How their hands shot up every time teachers asked questions, how when they answered, their voices were loud and sure.

We didn't know the kinds of things they knew, the kinds of things they taught at school. Waste of time, book-learning, our fathers said. What we needed to know was mapped out in the skies and soil, fenced off into the acreages tilled by our fathers and our father's fathers, back on back through all the names inscribed in our family Bibles. We went to school because we were law abiding, because we were only girls. We went until we were old enough to drop out, or until the men in our families got so sick or frail that the law didn't matter so much any more.

We were curious about boys, but we never imagined they were curious about us. We didn't think they saw us, didn't think they thought of anything but themselves, but then there came that day when one of them stopped us as we were leaving school – or, rather, when one of them stopped Georgia.

The boy was standing there as we left the schoolyard, and he drew himself up when we tried to pass. We hesitated as his eyes skimmed over each one of us, and then he saw recognised Georgia, and picked her out with a nod. We stared at him as he stared at Georgia, and we started when he spoke.

'I was wondering, Georgia, if you'd like to go to the pictures with me tonight.' His voice sounded loud and confident, and his eyes flashed, dangerous and fox-like. The way he raised his chin gave us the impression that there was only one answer he was prepared to hear, that he was doing us a favour, somehow, by asking. We all turned to look at Georgia. Her mouth opened then closed, and her face was as red as beet flesh.

'I said, I was wondering if you'd like to go to the pictures.' He spoke more slowly this time, as if we were slow ourselves, and the presumption in his voice awakened something within us. We were ready to raise our own chins, push past him, walk towards home without looking back. After all, what would girls like us want with a boy so idle, a boy who wouldn't become a man until after he'd gone to more school than our men would ever see, until he'd come back with nothing but a fancy piece of paper to show for himself.

But then, Georgia did something we none of us expected. She cocked her head, folded her arms in front of her chest and said, 'Sure'. The boy didn't look surprised, just held his hand out, and before we knew what was happening, Georgia had stepped forward and taken it. We held our breath, but it didn't stop the inevitable: he wrapped his hand around hers. We saw a fire of triumph blaze in his eyes and it made us afraid.

We gaped at Georgia who had just moments ago seemed like one of us but who now seemed as exotic as the women who dance for money at the state fair. None of us said anything as the boy led her away, and neither of them said goodbye. Georgia didn't look at us, no not once, not even a glance. The two of them shed us like old skin.

We stood in the schoolyard, blinking. It felt as if something violent had occurred, as if a limb had been severed. There was an emptiness among us, an emptiness where Georgia's silence should have been, and we had no idea what to do about it.

So, we began to look at each other. We looked at each other like we'd never looked before. What was it about Georgia that was so different from the rest of us? What had made her stand out? Our eyes peeled away the sunburns, the sun-bleached hair, the rough fingers, the mended clothes, searching out differences. We absorbed each other's eyes, breasts, mouths, hips. We assessed our figures, compared our facial features. Without saying a word, we broke each other into more pieces than we could ever put back together, and we felt ourselves broken as well.

The walk back to our farms was silent. We were curious about boys, but now we were curious about other things as well, things we weren't ready to talk about. One by one, we peeled off, heading to our separate homes. Not one of us said goodbye.

When I got to my own farmstead, I thought of my mother and sisters preparing dinner, and I thought of my father and brothers at the pump, washing up after a long day outdoors. I felt alone but didn't want to go home, so instead, I climbed the dry stone fence my great- or great-great-grandfather had made, and I dropped down into the field now lined with row upon row of tall, proud, corn. Sweetness spilled from the plants, pungent like perfume, and their golden tassels waved in the wind like Georgia's hair.

I grasped an ear in my hand and snapped it off its stalk. It felt thick and heavy, and for some reason, my fingers trembled. I pulled back the silk and husk and looked at the creamy yellow kernels inside. I pierced one with my fingernail, and white, milky liquid spurt onto my hand. Something was shifting – something big, like the seasons. I thought about Georgia and I thought about all of us. I thought about things that were now ripe, ready for picking.

Ingrid Jendrzejewski grew up in Vincennes, Indiana, studied creative writing at the University of Evansville, then physics at the University of Cambridge. Her work has found homes in places like *The Los Angeles Review, The Conium Review, Litro, Inktears, Neutrons/Protons, Flash Frontier, Vine Leaves, The Liars' League London, concīs* and *The Mainichi*. Last year, she won Gigantic Sequins' Flash Non-fiction Contest and the A Room of Her Own Foundation's Orlando Prize for Flash Fiction; recently, she received the Bath Flash Fiction Award. Links to Ingrid's work can be found at www.ingridj.comand she occasionally tweets @LunchOnTuesday

CHERISE SAYWELL

Comfort

The doctor sits on my stool in the alley. I do not offer her tea right away. I squat beside her and tell how I do the chat in the doorway, show how I rise from my seat and draw back the curtain, display my room and its clean covered floor. She wants to know everything about what I do. She has come early so my trade will not be interrupted. I tell her it is okay to stay a while, but it being a Wednesday, I count on at least three husbands and they will begin calling before the factory shifts begin, before the market opens. We say *caller* if they come a little, *husband* if they come a lot. They must find me available or they will go elsewhere.

Here comes a husband now, the one with the lace-up shoes. Even on the hottest days he wears them. When he takes his relief, those shod feet stick out off the mattress, laces tied tight. He could take them off in my room, on my covered floor.

'Comfort,' he calls, slowing, 'Good morning.' He will not stop, not with the doctor here. 'I thought you had your room at the bottom of this alley,' he says.

'Yes,' I tell him. 'Welcome was in this room. But she has

gone now.'

'Maybe I will visit you later,' he says. 'I will come at lunch.'

'Okay,' I say.

He might come; he might change his mind. There are a lot of girls along this strip. There are many younger than me.

'Is he a customer?' Doctor asks.

'Maybe,' I say.

'Has he been to you before?'

'Yes.'

'Will he come back to see you today?'

'Not if you are here.'

'I am sorry, Ayo,' she says. 'I will pay you.'

'When you see me here,' I tell her, 'you must call me Comfort.' It is my name for this room, for the husbands, the callers. They pass early in the morning on their way to their work. I smile if I see them coming. I say, *Comfort, husband*. Or, *Comfort here for you*. We choose our own word or we take from someone gone – if there is no word then a move, maybe, or a gesture. That way the husbands can tell their friends, I go to *Comfort* when I go work in the factory, in the market. They can name the alley where *Comfort* can be found, or *Welcome,* or there was that one who clicked her tongue and winked. The one who clicked her tongue and winked is dead now.

At the end of the day I take my own name back – take it home to my own room where I live with my daughters not yet grown.

To this doctor, I say, 'If you had come to my room where I live with my daughters, then you could call me Ayo.'

She smiles. She needs to see where I work, not how I live. 'There are so many questions,' she says. 'We do not have to answer them all today.'

This room used to belong to Welcome but it is mine three months now. Forty shillings more than my old room where I worked for so many years. I wondered if the luck would stay here, especially after Welcome died. But Welcome said it would be lucky for me to have so much extra space – a bed and a stove. Everything was better in this new room, except that the floor was dirt. I purchased lino offcuts in the rag market, a piece at a time. Each day I had a coin spare, I bought another piece; I covered another patch of the floor. Now only under the bed is still dirt.

All week I work. Monday, Tuesday, Wednesday especially, Thursday, Friday, Saturday. Sunday I go to Mass and pray. I keep to myself and no one knows me, so they don't look at me and wonder. But those that know me here, they wonder, like this doctor. Why am I still alive when so many others are gone? And so do I wonder, like them.

'Do you see the same men? Different men?' Doctor asks.

'Many men,' I tell her, 'same and different.' I explain to her. 'A caller might come regular, become a husband, but then he could pass you by for a while. Better not to rise off your chair until you know that husband is going to stop at your door, smile maybe, flick his hand across the curtain, happy to pay for what you have to offer.'

'What do you offer?'

'Comfort,' I say, 'like my name. And a covered floor so his feet stay clean for when he goes to work after.'

She smiles. Maybe not the answer she wanted. She wants to know about my service. What do I do that is different? What is the magic that guards my blood?

'Do your husbands go to the other girls often?' she asks.

'Yes,' I tell her.

'Do they go to any of the girls who visit the clinic?' We all use the clinic where this doctor works. No medicine at the government clinic.

'Of course,' I say.

One of my husbands went to Welcome for a while. She was young, fifteen years less than me. Who can blame him? He went to her once, twice, then every week for all spring. Then she was too busy to see him. And after that she was sick. So he came to me regular again for a while and then he did not come at all any more. But I am still here. So many years and I am still here. If the body cannot be saved then why does God save mine? My fame goes before me. My mystery.

Where does my luck come from? God? Some unknown sorcery? Or maybe just fate. The doctors want my blood. If they can look at it they might find an answer, they will be saviours.

The husbands, the callers, they do not think of luck, only relief – their brief forgetting.

I think of my pay and what must be purchased. Food, rent, kerosene. I pray my luck will keep.

Doctor would like to look in my room now. I have swept the floor so she can remove her shoes. If my luck leaves me this room will be big enough to live in, though not big enough for my daughters. They would have to stop school, go to work.

I show the doctor the Bible words on my wall. I got it at church. 'Proverb of Solomon,' I say.

'Can you read it?' the doctor asks.

'My daughters read for me,' I say. *'Hard Work is its Own Reward'*.

I like these words. I am not afraid of hard work. Each morning I fill the pan at the stand pump so I can wash when the work is done. Then I go for more water and I light the kero stove and boil it for the tea. I change into my bright work wrap while my tea steeps. It helps to cover myself with something cheery. It says I got the time to think about such things. I lie down on my mattress even a dozen times a day and my washcloth is always rinsed and hung so I can clean myself after. I attend to every detail. Each time I sweep the floor I get down on my hands and knees to check the lino pieces have not slipped.

Now I light the burner and boil water for tea. With the door-curtain pinned open the flies will come in so I leave it hanging shut even though the stove will make the room hot. I bring the seat inside. I place it where the doctor will not see that under the bed is still dirt. I have only one cup. I check it is perfectly clean.

'Thank you,' the doctor says.

Beside the door in a little box are the sheaths they give us at the clinic. 'Do you use these?' she asks.

'Sometimes,' I tell her. 'But if I am offered more shillings to go without, then I do.'

'Often?'

'Only if the man wishes it.'

Her brow creases. She touches a finger to her lip.

Some girls sell their sheaths in the market. Welcome did. I spare the doctor this fact.

When they first brought their clinic to our district the doctors told us women to act together in this matter. Unite, they advised us, and tell these men what they cannot have. But the doctors did not understand how it is for us, for the husbands, the callers. Heads or tails – our next breath clouds one side of a coin. That coin, when exchanged, is warm in our hand with the heat of a body, the thought of a meal. We are hungry all of us, and the men are so lonely, especially in the middle of the week. If they have a wife away in a village then they maybe miss her comfort. They stop on their way to work in the factory or the market. There are so many days until the end-of-week journey out of the city and home. You know it in their body and how they have you. You need the mattress hard so they do not hurt you. But even if they are rough they are silent so as not to disturb the next-door room. Sometimes a family stays there. The baby cries, the children play, and you hear it.

What the husbands and callers ask for, we give them. Together we move into our future one step at a time, each seeking to forget what runs behind us, its hot breath at our necks. We share that coin, and the burden of its brief release.

I give this doctor her tea.

'Do the men seem ill when they come to you?' she asks. 'Do you notice?'

'No,' I tell her. 'This sickness, it hides itself.'

'I know,' she says. 'But do the men ever ask about your health?'

'No,' I say. 'No chitter-chatter. It costs more to stay longer.'

'How many men?' Doctor asks. 'How many husbands? Callers?'

So many questions. 'On a Wednesday?'

'No. Altogether.'

'In a week?'

She lowers her voice for this shameful question. 'How many men since you began this work?'

I keep my tongue behind my teeth and my lip in front. In the café, do you count the cups of tea you make? Do you count the bowls of cornmeal you serve day after day? Do you count the plates you wash in the house of the mistress? Or the shirts you fold in the factory?

But I know that this question is not for shame. I say to the doctor, 'I cannot count how hard I work.'

She drinks some more tea and then she puts the cup down. She takes her pencil. She asks, how many days, how many years? How many husbands? How many callers on a good day, on a slow day? And I tell her and she writes down a big number. She shakes her head. What is my magic? For me, only those shillings. Rent. Food – tea and beans, cornmeal, rice. Kerosene to light the stove and cook. I send my daughters to school, each one. I will do this until they are grown – my only comfort.

God cannot save the body. This they tell us at church. So many girls. Their tongues go white. They cough and cough. They get thin. Then thinner. They work until they are too sick to work anymore.

The doctor tells me her science will explain my aberration. But I know well what they believe: that my body knows this sickness because it sees it so much. It does not open the door because it knows the wrong sound of the knock. It knows the face of that bad stranger. This doctor will not give me too many shillings. Because if I work less then maybe my body will forget and open the door without a thought.

The doctor finishes the tea I have made her. She puts the mug on the sill. 'What do you look forward to?' she asks me.

'I like to sweep my floor in the mornings,' I tell her. 'I like the feel of the lino when it is clean under my feet.'

'When you go to church, what do you pray for?'

'For a little more time,' I tell her. 'A little more work. Enough to keep my daughters in school.'

I never sell my sheaths. I gift them so my luck will keep. At church the preacher says our body is a temple, the temple of the Holy Spirit, but I know my body is only a little room with lino pieces to cover the dirt floor. It gives me no comfort to say God chooses for me to live through this.

Now the doctor counts out coins – a modest amount. She gives me a packet of tea. She clasps my hands. 'That is enough for today,' she says. 'We will see you at the clinic. Come in for anything you need.' Then she steps into her shoes, puts my stool by the door, and leaves.

I take my seat. Here come the husbands now, the callers. For each, I will remove my wrap and lie back. Arms up. No clasping. No embrace. I will look at the pictures Welcome left on the wall – a bird, a castle near water with trees around, an aeroplane flying over – and I will look on the words of Solomon.

Cherise Saywell was born and brought up in Australia and lives in Scotland. She has published two novels, *Desert Fish* (2011) and *Twitcher* (2013 – both Vintage). Her short stories have won the Mslexia Short Story Prize and the V.S. Pritchett Prize and been shortlisted for the Asham Award and the Salt Prize. Last year she had a story selected for BBC Radio 4 *Opening Lines*. Cherise's stories have been published in *Mslexia, The London Magazine* and *New Writing Scotland,* as well as several anthologies. She is working (and working and working) on her third novel.

RUPERT DASTUR

White Flags

I'm chugging gin like an old truck running on apocalypse fuel, my knock-out breath wheezing past ribs that rattle more than danger. Fact is, I've got a little fear in my belly and not one person will believe the cause – not my Marie, not the fellas, not a soul on this goddamned earth.

I'm a fifty-three year old man, carrying sixteen stones, with fists that have knocked out more teeth than a crocodile jaw, and I'm scared of shadows and strangers. I've taken to praying. Every day I get down on my knees, bring my hands together and say the Lord's Prayer just as I did when I was a kid and mam whispered behind me asking forgiveness for our sins. If she was here she'd say pull yourself together – speak to one of the fathers. Absolve yourself. But I've said my Hail Marys and done my time before the cross; nothing will shake the truth.

Yesterday I spent the whole afternoon at St. Matthew's; when I got home at eight, Marie put an empty plate in front of me and said God's not listening or doesn't care and either way you need to get going or we'll be skin and bones and meeting Him sooner than we should. I tried to explain things but she started shouting, rubbing her hands through her hair, face red and scared and angry, the plate flying through the air and smashing against a cupboard, the little pieces scattering like shot from a gun.

Marie is finding the situation difficult and she's asked for help – first from Father John and then from Our Sal whose brother is part of the network and some kind of doctor. I tried to calm Marie down, tell her I'm not crazy, but she just looks at me like she's thinking of packing a suitcase. She's already taken the kids to Aunt G's.

There was no trigger warning when O'Donoghue appeared like the very thing he was. I was walking back from Christie's – before I lost the job – when I *felt* something and turned around and saw him standing there, with the same smile he had ten years ago and the hole in his forehead where I'd sent a 6mm to end a host of suspicions.

Sure, my heart leapt up like a startled dog and my palms were all sweat, but I had to know. O'Donoghue? I said. In reply he turned around and walked away. I traced his steps but he lost me after a few twists and turns down Kilburn, disappearing like ash in wind.

This happened four times before I cracked and told Marie after a bottle of help. She said it was the guilt, wasted though it was on a son of a whore. I was going soft, she said. I told her that I'd made my peace long ago. Besides, we were friends, even at the end. My wife sent a missile of spittle to the floor. To that traitor? Her brows crouching down like a cat.

O'Donoghue and I had grown up together; same street, same school, same church. Our mams were thick together, sisters in arms, and we were brothers in all but blood. He was a clever kid and that was his problem. I warned him about it, all those years ago. Talking tongues lead to broken bones, I said. He could have joined the cloth, but as things were we both signed up to the cause. I wish to God he'd picked up the white collar rather.

The Doc's a comrade and so I'm free to speak about the

past and family, though I don't tell him everything, of course. I can't see what good all this talk will do, but Our Sal's pulled a favour and Marie has given the ultimatum. She's started working shifts at the local and has stopped speaking to me. I can't read what's in her eyes now and something about that frightens me more than any number of words.

I tried to talk about the kids the other day and she held up her hand and said if I dare go near them. I called her names like I did when we were first married and I had to hide politics. She turned all wood, like her feet had roots buried in the ground, not a flinch as I raised my hand. I didn't touch her though. I'd never do that. I just can't stop thinking about my kids and O'Donoghue and the next drink.

Doc's a passive sort of man, but sits big behind the desk, his hands clasped together like he's trying to keep back his thoughts. I tell him what happened all those years ago and he just sits there, head bobbing up and down like he's heard everything before. I give him the recent facts. How I had seen O'Donoghue sixteen times in the last three months. How he's always dressed the same, never speaks, just looks at me. Doc mentions the Macbeth effect, but I tell him again and again that I have washed my hands of blood. There's not a speck, I say. Not a speck. He tells me to stay off the spirits. I tell him I'm four days dry.

Marie's helping with the drink. I'm shaking, but going clean and strong. Last weekend I saw Jack and little Grace, their faces all wide-eyed and grinning. We went to the park, pushing the swings higher and higher, Jack and Grace sending shrieks into the air, right up to the heavens. We were mid-push when I saw O'Donoghue at the edge of the green. He waved at me and without thinking I raised my own arm in reply. Daddy, said Grace, her shining eyes looking down. Marie, who was standing behind Jack, glanced over. Mickey, she said. I told them it was nothing, suddenly feeling happy – really happy –

for the first time in a long while. I could handle this.

When I said goodbye at Aunt G's, Grace asked me when they could come back home. Soon, I said. She wrapped her arms around my neck and said I love you Daddy, and then she started crying. I kissed her and promised it wouldn't be long. I then looked up at Marie and she gave the smallest of nods which felt like the raising of a white flag. I had experienced too much to believe in peace, but so long as the guns were lowered there was hope.

O'Donoghue and I joined the cause as young recruits, full of naïve ideals. It didn't take long for the chill of disillusion to set in, but by then the uniform was the only thing keeping us warm. Gradually suits replaced soldiers, but there was still a network of blood leading all the way to London. In order to manoeuvre between the minefield, information and broken bones were needed, for a few years O'Donoghue and I were considered the greenest of cadets in more ways than one. As papers were signed beneath desks, we were sent out to silence whispers – to shake up those who weren't happy with the changing circumstances.

The English drove hard deals, despite post-box bombs, as if they knew things they shouldn't. Rumours surfaced about O'Donoghue. Evidence lined up; quiet as a mole beneath the ground he had been snuffling out secrets and passing them to the enemy. He was accused of derailing the fight for independence. Top command wanted him gone and I was tasked with proving my loyalty.

O'Donogue knew what was coming when I turned up at his home. We shared a drink. A toast to white flags, he said. I had another drink. It's a hard thing to raise the barrel of a gun to a friend.

Forgetting where I am and who I'm with, I narrate all this to the Doc who sits with his brown eyes set behind thick-rimmed glasses. He wasn't married, I noticed. He couldn't know how much I love my kids and the lengths I would go to see them safe.

What do you mean white flags, asks the Doc. I shrug. He tells me it was a difficult business. He asks if I have seen O'Donoghue recently. My ghostly companion. I said I had, but it was manageable. I had things under control. Well brother, he says, I sure hope so.

I don't like his tone and ask him what the hell he means by that. He leans back in his chair, pulls out an envelope from a drawer and passes it over. Trouble is gathering, he says, momentum for the cause is picking up again and we don't need talk of ghouls and goblins. You know the network is still active, he says. Of course I fucking do, I reply, my hand ripping open the lip of the envelope. I look at the photographs of my wife and children.

If I had been younger I would have lifted the glass paperweight on his desk and buried it into the side of his skull. We're done here, aren't we, I say. He nods and I shake his hand and call him brother.

The chaos of children has returned to the house and as I stroll back to Warwick Street I feel a tightening in my chest as I think of the danger that surrounds them at every moment of their lives. Down each street and road lurks some new evil and there are no maps to guide a spirit through the labyrinth of history and all its violence and deception. If I had wealth and time I would lay a yellow brick road for my daughter and son, a path that was safe and whole and led to whatever good place awaits us. But this is fantastical thinking. Not far from here are politicians and businessmen who brought trouble to this island, who plundered and murdered with pen and paper; the same men who would sacrifice a new generation for an old cause. I turn around and see John O'Donoghue, truth in the eyes of the dead that follow my footsteps.

It's Sunday afternoon and the church bells are ringing. We walk outside as a family, the first service we've attended together since my past rose up from the ground and my hand reached for the bottle. I ask Marie to take the kids with her. It's okay, I say, I won't be long. I survey the garden of the dead, bones next to bones under earth and stone. I find O'Donoghue's grave, the writing still too fresh, the dates too close together.

He walks up to me and I return his smile. There's trouble coming, John, I say. He nods slowly. You can feel it, hissing beneath the seeming calm, ready to boil up, to rise up, a new world of men and women too young to appreciate compromise.

My nephew, says O'Donoghue, you'll take care of him? You know I will, I reply. I look at the hole drilled into my friend's brow like a third eye. He is twenty-one years old. I cannot believe we were ever so dark-haired, unwrinkled, undone. I tell him I'm sorry and he shrugs, says we did what we had to. Traitors both, one of us had to hang. I ask him if he thinks we picked the right side. It's better than red streets, he echoes across the years.

I ask him what it's like and he shakes his head, smiling. There are always rules, he says. I tell him I have to get back to my family and he nods and then salutes.

I walk away, feeling his eyes on my back. I think about my contacts and the channels of communication still open in England. There is trouble coming. The Doc knows it, O'Donogue knows it, and I know it. Nations are cracking, breaking up, the young searching for themselves among the boredom and poverty, too peaceful to know the feel of a gun pressed against skin, their only violence stuck behind the safe excitement of a screen.

I look back, but O'Donoghue has disappeared among his own. I search for the car and spot Marie standing next to our Fiat, our children sticking their heads out of the wound-down windows, smiling as they wave, their beautiful unblemished hands like white flags in the wind.

Rupert Dastur is a writer and freelance editor. He is director of *The Short Story,* an online platform for short fiction news, views, and competitions. More details can be found at www.theshortstory.co.uk. His most recent work is forthcoming in *A3 Review, New Flash Fiction Review,* and *Bath Flash Fiction Anthology 2016*.

CLARE REDDAWAY

Avocet

I am a twitcher. There, I've said it. I've *confessed.* Do I feel better? No. Why would I? I know you'll be judging me. It's not cool. Not urban. Not metrosexual or arty or down-with-da-kidz. I'm not watching an installation of a dead cow in a white gallery in Soho, I'm watching blue tits nesting in a suburban magnolia. I'm not – OK, you get it. Birds. I'll watch anything. A thrush, her throat speckled and pulsing, warbling in the dawn light. A buzzard gliding on a hot air current rising from the city. An opportunistic crow feasting on roadkill. I like – well, do you want to know what I like best? An avocet.

When I was very small my father brought me home an avocet. It was a picture, printed on that never-ending computer paper with perforations on the sides, the kind you don't get anymore. The bird was made out of black Xs. It was standing on one leg, the other tucked up, bent at the knee joint. It had a short neck and a long beak curved upwards like a spoon but reed slender, not wide. It was black and white. Well, the Xs were black and the paper was white and later it turned out that was an accurate depiction of an avocet, and not deceptive, like the telly.

'Wow,' I said. 'How did you do *that*?'

My father was grinning and shifting from foot to foot with excitement.

'On a computer,' he said.

I had no idea what he meant.

'What's a computer?' I asked.

In my defence, no-one had computers in those days and I was only six. My father was now hopping from foot to foot.

'It's a very clever machine, sweetie, that helps Daddy in his work.'

Now my mother smiled.

'Who drew it?'

Why did she always do that? Why did she make him scowl?

'The computer.'

'It's a picture. Is that what the computer is supposed to do?'

'We're trialling -'

'So who drew it?'

'We're trialling new software -'

'Who drew it!'

'It's a picture! Of a bird! For God's sake! It's for Elly, for a child, for my daughter!'

'Who -'

'A colleague! A friend. A friend who is a colleague.'

'How kind of her.'

'I thought so.'

'Elly, sweetie, you and William pop upstairs and find Mummy's reading glasses. There's a piece in the paper I want to show Daddy.'

My mother's eyes were shiny, and my father was staring fixedly at his finger which was carefully tracing the avocet's wing on the computer paper, round and round, back and forth. We left the room.

'Gran says it'll be a bleeding miracle,' said my brother, taking the stairs two at a time.

'What will?'

'If their marriage lasts. A bleeding miracle.'

I pictured Gran, cigarette hanging off her bottom lip, Guinness in hand. Her face was one big wrinkle. I could imagine her saying that.

'Lalalalalalalala,' I sang, putting my fingers in my ears.

'Bleeding miracle, bleeding miracle, bleeding miracle,' sang my brother, peeling my fingers away from my ears, one at a time.

Under the circumstances you wouldn't think that the avocet would be my favourite would you. I should hate them, link them forever with the moment that my mother confronted my father about his mistress. Well, you'd be wrong.

That summer we went to Suffolk on holiday as usual. My brother and I shared a bunk bed the size of our bedroom in the pink-washed cottage where the walls were thick enough and old enough to swallow the tears and recriminations of my parents in the room next door. We spent our days shivering on a pebbly beach, salvaging rope and driftwood, and swimming in the icy grey North Sea.

One afternoon, when the drizzle was too heavy to pretend that the beach was fun, my father took me for a walk. 'He's chosen me, he's chosen me,' I hummed as we wound our way along a sandy path across the heathland at the top of the cliffs, through purple heather and waist-high bracken, to a hide made of logs. We climbed inside. There was no window, but a long open slit like a letter box, on one wall. My father took two pairs of binoculars out of his knapsack. We settled down on the bench, binoculars resting on the edge of the opening. It took to me a while to focus the lenses, but at last I managed.

The tide was out. I could see mudflats the colour of milky tea with pewter pools of standing water. I could see sand, shaped into ripples by retreating waves. I could see birds.

Long red legs, red beak, imperious – a redshank.

A stockier bird, clad in dapper black and white suit –

'Oyster catcher,' my father whispered.

Scudding across the flats like wind on water, camouflaged as mud, visible only by their movement and their black patched bellies – a family of dunlins.

I followed swarms of birds with my binoculars, watched them fly, land, walk, stare, turn, preen, dip their beaks into the mud, pull out worms, catch insects on the wing. I saw their reflections wet upon the wet mud. I saw them twist their heads and stretch their wings and I saw their beauty, their elegance, their grace. They were wild and free and they were a hand's width away.

We stayed in the hide for hours. Eventually, I began to tire. I was hungry, stiff, thirsty and I wanted to wee. I dragged at my father's sleeve.

'Patience,' he said, and his binoculars scanned the mud, back and forth, up and down.

'What are you looking for?' I asked, but I knew.

'I'm hoping for an avocet,' he said. As he stared out, he told me their history. Black and white birds with elegant speckled eggs, so prized by Victorian schoolboys and Victorian egg collectors that their nests were raided and raided and raided again until there were no more avocets, and they became extinct in the British Isles. But now there were stories that they had returned. That if you were clever or still and silent or very very lucky you could see an avocet pair foraging on the Suffolk mudflats.

I could scarcely breathe. Would we see them? Could we? I too stared out, raking the mudflats, straining to hear the *thweep thweep thweep* of the bird. We stayed until the tide came in and swept away the waders' pools, and vanished the mudflats until morning.

'Spying. Why do you need to do it in your spare time too? I suppose that's all you're good for. Don't you get her into it. It's a dirty business,' said my mother as she slammed down the supper, dried out and caked from waiting. My father winked at me. I smiled.

What was dirty about bird watching? I wondered, but like many of the things she said this rolled over and out of my head. I was absorbed in drawing the wings of a gull. I was flaring the tail feathers and colouring in the yellow eye. I was trying to remember the exact hook of the beak. I didn't think my mother meant anything. It wasn't until later that I found out my father didn't use the computer purely to draw birds to entertain his daughter, nor did he use it only to flirt with his mistress – but rather to analyze the data captured from thousands upon thousands of recorded telephone conversations from oblivious members of the public.

I didn't learn this until later, when my brother again prized my fingers away from my ears.

I didn't like it, I didn't like it at all. I was marching in protests and burning my bra and banning the bomb and chaining myself to anything that would have me and many things that wouldn't. It didn't fit with my world view. My establishment father? My father who'd programmed the computers that the spies used? The establishment spies. The enemy.

Odd to stop talking to your father because of politics. Because you don't approve of his choice of career. Odd – unless you realize that of course that's not why you've stopped, it's just what you've chosen to give yourself as the reason. It's the easiest reason, one that has no ties of hurt. 'He's too right wing' is so much easier than 'he didn't love me enough to stay.'

Because my father was long gone by then of course. Gran was right. It would have been a bleeding miracle if that marriage had survived, even though divorce was frowned on and my mother wasn't sure that living on her own was better than living with a philanderer. So she found herself another one, and settled down warily, careful not to ask too many questions this time.

My father carried on trying with me. He'd send letters. He wouldn't tell me about his new marriage, his new children. He wouldn't ask me about my life, my job, my lovers. He'd send me his logs of his birds.

Minsmere. 29th April. A family of lapwings. Shelducks. I heard a curlew but didn't spot it. A pair of black-tailed godwits!

And *Colonsay. September.* (What was he doing in Scotland?) *Lots of kittywakes and guillemots. Did catch a storm petrel on the wing! Perhaps he was blown off course?*

The last one just said: *At last! I've spotted one, for definite! Couldn't believe it! Beautiful!* He didn't need to tell me what he'd seen.

I didn't answer. I never answered. The patience that he showed while waiting for his birds, the patience he showed while sifting through the reams and reams of data, that patience, that perseverance, that dogged endurance ran out. He withdrew, politely, without a fuss, without a battle, and he waited. But I had inherited that patience and his stubbornness. I could have told him about my birds. The condors, wild and huge, swooping over the Andes, with their strange fingered wing tips. The bird of paradise I saw in the Indonesian jungle, its tail as twirled as Dali's moustache. The turquoise flash of the kingfisher by the river where I walk my dog. I didn't tell him.

I didn't even go to his funeral.

Now that I am old, the anger and the hurt have vanished, and I can't forgive myself. I can't let it go. It's too late to make my peace and now I can't remember why I started the war.

So all these years later, I'm trying to cauterize the wound. I'm following his log. I find myself in a hide in Minsmere in Suffolk, exactly where we'd been that first time.

I thought that it would be hours, days maybe. But I raised my binoculars to my eyes and I saw – avocets. Maybe as many as twenty pairs. As I watched, a chick emerged out onto the mudflats for the first time, hesitant, a little shivery, staying close to its mother, learning to follow, learning to feed, learning to live. I was looking through my lenses at a Lazarus species, raised from the dead. I was witnessing my own living fluffy tottering miracle.

And it came to me, not in a blinding flash or with a fanfare of trumpets, but as gently as a sea mist – it didn't matter. My father knew that one day I'd follow his letters. That I'd go in his footsteps and that I would, like him, see my avocet. And I'd understand.

I didn't wipe out a whole species of birds. I just didn't say goodbye to my father. But I still could.

So I did.

And as I did, the chick put its beak into the water and started to feed itself for the very first time.

Clare Reddaway loves stories: writing them, reading them, listening to them, eavesdropping on them. She has read her stories to anyone who will listen at events and festivals around the south of England, for years. Her stories do get published and win competitions sometimes. She runs Story Fridays, a regular live literature event in Bath, to share the story-love. She also writes scripts, and a number of her plays have been performed and recorded recently. You can find out more about her work – and hear some of her stories at www.awordinyourear.org.uk

WILLIAM SHIH

Mrs. Li

Mrs. Li has waited many days for this day to finally come — she is quite sure it is the day of her death. She is lying on her bed, her salt and pepper curls drenched in sweat. She can feel someone digging through the pockets of her pants, then rummaging underneath her cheap cotton shirt, her sweatshop's castaway. But it is only Ah Leung, her eldest. Her son's fingers pass over her dry skin. They are rough. They are coarse. He is patting her down. She murmurs for him to move, tells him that he is blocking her light, the dusty fixture hanging from the cracked ceiling above. It is then that her son finds what he is looking for. He takes her wallet, tucks it into the pocket of his jeans. He removes her jewelry. Gold that she wears for luck. Pearls, for some semblance of her youth. One by one, he tosses her belongings into a red plastic shopping bag that reeks of melted meat, of fish from the markets, the sharp and metallic sweet stench of blood. Mrs. Li then grabs ahold of her jade, her bracelet. She strengthens her grip.

'Bu, bu.' She shakes her head, long arthritic fingers coiled around her thick wrist. She begs her favorite child — for being born first and for being born a boy — not to take the good luck charm, but he does so anyway.

'Better safe than sorry,' Ah Leung says. 'One never knows with nurses.'

It is somehow decided—her daughter's family will finish eating dinner first. Then they will leave Brooklyn for Chinatown, for Manhattan. They will drive Mrs. Li to the hospital, only blocks away. It is rumored that ambulances are only free of charge when the patients are unconscious — or so the family understands. There is even some talk that it may be better to wait until that happens, if it happens.

'We shall see,' she hears Ah Leung say over the phone.

It's been a week since Mrs. Li's left her Mott Street apartment. Even longer since she's been invited to visit her daughter's family, taken the D train to Bensonhurst. But she can still picture their rosewood cherry dining table. At one end, her youngest daughter, Ah Ling, a seamstress at a sweatshop. An already greying husband who drives trucks, sitting beside her. Two teenage boys, situated across the table, both in college. One Mrs. Li can't help favoring over the other because centuries of tradition has deemed it so — the eldest, Jackson. He is the taller of the two, thankfully. Rougher skinned, which can't be helped. Broader shoulders, perhaps a bit too much rice. But his wide forehead means that he is astute and wise. Mrs. Li can see the small television set blinking over the family's heads. TVB, the Hong Kong station. A dramatic series, unrequited love set in the Tang or Ming or Qing Dynasty. Over the table, the spread of dinner. Roast pork, tilapia, cabbage so green. Unfinished bowls of rice. Bird's nest soup to be drunk at the end of meals, so savory, bitter as medicine. Mrs. Li can't help swallowing, though her mouth is dry. She can almost taste the concoction, the sharpness of the ginger, the salt. Her daughter has never been known for her cooking.

Then nausea overtakes Mrs. Li. She hasn't had an appetite

for weeks. Spells of lightheadedness, headaches that come and go, that seize her when she least expects them.

'Lack of iron!' Mrs. Wong from the senior citizen center had figured before sharing some of her anti-inflaming pills. 'Good to put out internal heat.'

Last Tuesday, Mrs. Li had actually fainted. Lucky that Ah Leung had been there to catch her. Lucky that he had brought her the expired aspirin, so as not to waste it. But what was that look in his face? Was it a kind of expectation? Did she detect the slightest hint of impatience, eagerness? Yes, she did. Mrs. Li is well aware: her family has been readying themselves for years. Her plot on Mount Pleasant in White Plains, already paid for—Ah Ling had compared it to buying prime real estate. Good daughter. The preparations at Wah Wing Sang Funeral Corporation on Mulberry, already settled. All the white flowers, practically waiting to be picked.

'Aiya, Ma,' Mrs. Li can hear Ah Leung say, see him scrunch his flat nose as he pushes himself off the spring mattress. 'When was the last time you bathed?'

'Pains,' Mrs. Li moans, her voice croaky, weakening with each passing second. 'Can't breathe. My life is fading.'

There is a kind of gratification in embracing death on one's own terms.

She watches her son shake his head. From the inner pocket of his windbreaker, he pulls out his expensive camera and starts to peruse his most recent photographs. Since Ah Leung's retired from the restaurant, he's fancied himself a photographer. The fountain at Lincoln Center, fields at Central Park. F.A.O. Schwartz selling toys that he's never thought to buy for his own children. Photography, such a self-indulgent endeavor, Mrs. Li can't help but think, a waste of time, of energy. Worst of all, a waste of money. She watches the back of his balding head, even as she continues to moan.

'Oh, my son. My precious son.'

He turns around. The bluish light from the camera reflects

a consternated face, thick drooping lips, squinting intelligent eyes that have always reminded Mrs. Li of her husband, Fong Yet—dead now. Ten years. A second stroke.

After her husband's first stroke, doctors had prohibited him from traveling abroad. It was she who had gone back to their village in Hoishan, Pearl River Delta, China. There was a duty to fulfill—an obligatory outdoor banquet under the setting sun for the distant relatives. People she no longer recognized. Faces so wrinkled by the sun, backs so hunched from tending farms, or fishing in the manmade lake. Smiles, missing and rotting teeth. The red envelopes that Mrs. Li had had to dole out as if she were a bank. How she detested so much of it, but it had to be done. To save face. Because to return from America meant something—it meant that one had to obscure the truth. It meant an obligation to uphold the belief that a better life was only an ocean away, even long after one realized that this wasn't exactly true. Because to be Hoishanese meant to be second class, worse — to be silent in the face of injustice, to be able to hold one's tongue always, always to hope for the benefit of the doubt, for a returning gesture of kindness.

To work so hard, and still to never belong. Then, to watch your children not belong, and their children as well.

To watch them all turn around, blame one for this fate. It is all too much for a single person to take, and yet, she takes it and takes it.

That evening. The ten round banquet tables. The boisterous chatter of her village tongue. Communal laughter that she hadn't heard in what felt like a lifetime. Ji-ji, ja-ja, ji-ji, ja-ja. It almost made her visit worth the price of the plane ticket, the fare for the bus from Hong Kong, the inconvenience of having to risk her life, rumors of being kidnapped and held for ransom once she passed inspection at Shenzhen.

'Must be so rich, so lucky, so happy,' a woman who had claimed to be a cousin's cousin had called out to Mrs. Li from an adjacent round table. Several relatives had turned expectantly towards her.

'Oh, yes,' Mrs. Li had said. 'You must come one day and see for yourself.'

A flash goes off. Ah Leung is taking her picture. She tells him to stop, but he takes another, then another.

'No,' Mrs. Li mutters. 'Bad luck.' Then again, no such thing as bad luck anymore. This is it.

She utters one more wish, more than once, before Ah Leung pays her any attention.

'Just one more.'

What she would have given just to be there for her husband when he'd fallen in the bathroom. How many hours had he laid there, heat drifting from his body until there was no more heat, but that eternal coldness.

Mrs. Li has always believed it to be her fault. How it's haunted her. Years. She'd rather be haunted by his ghost, but even his ghost has seemed to abandon her. But no more. She will join her husband. She will see him in the afterlife.

'Let me spend my last moments here,' she pleads. 'This is my home.'

Her fingers reach out. Her parched lips quiver.

'Aiya Ma!' her son snaps. 'Relax, okay?'

She closes her eyes, takes a breath. 'No one wants to die in a hospital.'

Moments later. There is a pounding at the door. Mrs. Li figures that it is only her daughter, Ah Ling, who has come to retrieve her. But so soon? Mrs. Li wonders if she is losing her own sense of time. To her surprise, it is not her daughter. Instead, she hears the voices of men. Brutal, assertive English, and they are drawing closer. Ah Leung's voice has changed. He has lost his authority as he tries desperately to dissuade the men from coming inside.

Then the two EMS men barge into her room. They are young, fit. They move determinedly. Ah Leung utilizes his broken phrases and pseudo-sign-language in an effort to let them know, they are not needed here.

'Sir,' one of the men says to Ah Leung, 'step aside, please.' He is tall and black, muscular. Too young to be called a man, skin so smooth, not a wrinkle across his chiseled face.

'Wan dan le,' Ah Leung mutters under his breath. Oh now he's done it.

'Who?' Mrs. Li murmurs. 'Who has done it?'

'Who do you think?' Then, 'Jackson, your grandson.'

She shakes her head in response.

'He's called the ambulance, Ma!'

'Aiya.' That Jackson should know better. Has he already forgotten that the Chinese just want to be left alone? The Middle Kingdom, the Forbidden City. The Great Wall.

The men's hands are covered with baby blue gloves. They dig into her flesh; the last of Mrs. Li's strength fails her. But she relies on her best asset — her weight. She allows herself to sink into the bed. Deeper, deeper. Still, they somehow manage to lift her. It's actually rather easy for them. These men must be accustomed to carrying dead bodies, Mrs. Li thinks. Even fat ones, like hers. But how humiliating to be taken out of her apartment like this, seated on a chair as if it were a human sedan, carried through the damp hallway, down two flights of stairs for all to see. She imagines Mr. Yuang from down the hall, always spying through the peephole of his apartment, whispering absurdities to his wife. 'Who does she think she is?' Mrs. Li can imagine him saying, 'a Qing princess?'

Such misunderstandings, the seeds of gossip.

The bottom of the steps. The ambulance waiting in front. The two EMS men lay her on a stretcher. They tie her up, wrap an oxygen mask over her glistening face, full of pocks.

'Breathe,' the black man tells her. Her son translates. 'Come on, breathe.'

But to her horror, the commotion has attracted the attention of what looks to be all of Chinatown. Sirens, rotating red and blue lights, like an overture to a summer evening show. Mrs. Li, the star. She is mortified. She shields her face with a hand, but can't help noticing Mrs. Wang in the crowd wearing a robe and slippers, arms crossed against her tiny chest. Beady eyes, snake that she is. Aiya. Tomorrow the woman will be sure to tell everyone at Columbus Park.

All the fortunetellers there will say they saw it coming.

Flat on her back. The hospital. New York Downtown. Mrs. Li is wheeled into the cold ER lobby. The air conditioning is on, even at such an hour. Immediately, Mrs. Li understands. It is where they take all the elderly of her neighborhood—where they took her husband. After all these years, the hospital has yet to acquire someone who can speak the jagged dialect of Hoishanhua. The good-for-nothing Mandarin and Cantonese translator offers his services; a middle-aged man with glasses smiles hopelessly. Doesn't anyone remember? It was the Hoishanese who built and sustained all the Chinatowns across the Americas. Twenty years ago, if one didn't speak Hoishanhua, one couldn't even buy a fish.

Oh, Fong Yet. Get me out of here. Mrs. Li thinks of how the doctors couldn't communicate with her family. They had asked her grandson, Jackson, to translate. Back then, he was only ten. What else could he do but cry and cry? So it comes full circle, Mrs. Li realizes. Yin-yang, but more than simply round — everything interpenetrated. She feels chills. She is feverish. She feels queasy. She wonders how the spirits will treat her when they receive her. Will they welcome her? Or will they punish her?

The pale fluorescent beams barely offer a glimmer of hope. The ER corridor smells of antiseptic and plastic, the mustiness of the elementary school cafeteria where she goes to see performances during the Mid-Autumn Festival. Not quite clean.

Nurses bustle around her. She is being pushed through a succession of swinging doors. The bright lights pass overhead. They start to blur, brighten. They are glinting. They are suddenly akin to the flickering lamplights at dusk.

And then she is young again.

William Pei Shih is a graduate of the Iowa Writers' Workshop. His stories have been recognized by the John Steinbeck Fiction Award, the Bridport Prize, *The Masters Review* Short Story Award, the Raymond Carver Short Story Contest, the Alice Munro Short Story Competition, Matrix Magazine's Lit POP Award in Fiction, the AAWW/*Hyphen* Asian American Short Story Award, the Hemingway Short Story Competition, *Writer's Digest*, *Narrative Magazine*, and *Glimmer Train*. A Pushcart Prize Nominee, his stories have been published by *The Masters Review*, *Carve Magazine*, the *Bridport Prize Anthology*, *The Des Moines Register*, *Reed Magazine*, and *Hyphen*. He is a 2016 Sun Valley Writers' Conference Fellow.

JACKY TAYLOR

Searching for the Silver Darlings

When night comes, men become blind to squalls and waves as high as steeples – their quiet pockets and noisy bellies drive them to the sea.

This morning ten boats are already beached beneath the undercliff. Billy Gibbs barks at himself in disgust – first out, last back now is it? There are calls of *lost your touch eh Billy* and younger men, eager to be their own masters, asking if his boat's for sale. There'll be ribbing while the fish is sorted, words about the catch, his age, how better men are lining up to take his share.

He heaves and hauls *The Flighty Mary* up onto the shingle, turning the winch handle with muscle and fury, still the only man to land his boat single-handed. But it's taking more of him each time – the burn of metal scorching his palms, the arch of his back cracking under the strain.

The men lay wooden boxes row on row along the shore. Some are brimming with dun-cow, sprats and pilchards, but still no herring. Billy's missed the best of them to chase those silver darlings. So thin are the contents of his boxes he's propped them tail up to give more bulk, but they only look as if they are diving away in disdain.

Women from the village are already on the foreshore eyeing the fish, pinching flesh to weigh up how many it'll take to feed the gaping mouths at home, but money is scarce and a few heads is all some will buy. It's not enough to nourish bone or sinew, but will silence rumbling bellies for a day.

A woman with paper-skin hands points to the smallest fish in Billy's catch.

'How much?'

He knows she can't afford whatever he says, so he slips two pilchards into the pocket of her apron – for the littluns. She won't look him in the eye and turns away leaning into the wind too desperate to refuse and too ashamed to thank him.

He sells a few small pollack and bass from his thinnest box and empties the dregs of what's left back into the sea. Gulls swoop in from every direction tearing bloody pieces out of each other's beaks, splitting the sky with squabbling.

The women draw away, ebbing in their own tide of black and navy serge, nodding like buoys as they walk back to their cottages. The men follow, hauling boxes up onto their shoulders to load the donkey carts waiting at the bottom of Tin Hill. Billy Gibbs loads his too and if he was not so bent with contempt for himself he might have caught sight of someone watching him.

She's stood on Gull Head many times, seen Billy bring in *The Flighty Mary* by himself – his catch always the best, year on year. Sure they'd all scoff and jeer when he set his course for another part of the bay. *Nothing but weed there Billy Gibbs* they'd laugh and whoop, but faces would fall when he came back with a deck full of herring.

Is it just time falling on his shoulders that stunts his haul? The years bring creaking bones she's felt herself, cracking every tread when Winter air snaps like a tin trap. She can tell by the stoop of his back how much it bothers him and when the beach has emptied of all but himself, she's seen Billy Gibbs slide the back of his hand across his eyes. She's felt salt stinging her own.

But Lizzie Marshall won't buy fish today because her fingers would press the stink of it into her work and once in, she'd never get it out. She has handkerchief edgings to finish, a bonnet veil to complete and a christening robe to begin. She must stretch the finished panels of an altar cloth, easing them into shape as lacy fish swim within their borders. Her fingers must be fresh and faultless as bobbins fly between them, thread dancing lily-white over her pillow as pins hold each pattern in place. No, she has enough to last another day and there's only herself to feed now after all. She'll move about the village, listen at door cracks and casements, pause by the The Blue Anchor and turn her ear to tales. She'll match her pace to donkey feet and nod up Tin Hill as men blather. She'll sift truth from rumour as the ice-wind fingers her neck and stay closed and secret, knowing there are always jealous hearts where good souls lie.

And when dark falls between the houses, Lizzie will lay a nightshirt on her quilt. Folded in upon itself, she'll open up each crease. The collar on her pillow, the hem flapping at the end of the bed. Her feet will scuff and shuffle as she moves round to unwrap the sleeves and soon it will be lying like a flat, wingless angel. She'll cup her hands to her lips, open her palms and press the place where a man's heart should be. She'll fan her fingers over the creases, slide her hands along each sleeve, her body inching closer until she's climbed inside.

But this is not her dead husband's shirt, not the shroud of a man whose roughness scored her like glass. Nor the yellowing cotton she's seen hanging in other cottages, limp and lifeless on the back of bedroom doors. This is cloud-white and crisp, fresh as air on her skin with lace from her fingers. This is the shirt for a man father barred from his door and she'll wrap its emptiness around her, warm it to life as she rocks in its arms.

Billy is out checking his nets. The hemp has worn so thin in places you can barely see it, without repair it will split next time he casts and so little in his boxes means no new reel for mending. He must take his chances and hope the shoals will come and nets will hold. He looks over *The Flighty Mary*, slaps his palm against her bow, eyes the clinker planks for gaps and cracks. He runs his hand along her gunnels like a lover and his fingers linger in another time. Padding them against the grain he recalls frets of lace, feels the work of them on the side of his boat as his fingers bump over flakes of peeling paint.

His thumb remembers the petal-soft curve at the base of her throat, his hand the perfect fit of her cheek in the cup of it. And he looks out over the waves fixing his mind's eye on that day, feels his ribcage rise from the roar he has kept inside for years. He'll drive it back down, be a demon at his work, turn his heart to the wall. He'll be gruff and keep only his own company as he clings to his quest for herring.

In the split of light bridging night and day men are gathering on the shore, readying for the next haul. Some of the women are clustered like bags of shadows on Tin Hill, pinned to the place where there are always partings. Others have spilled their way down to the shingle beach, eager to tread the same ground as their sweethearts for as long as they can. When the boats have set sail, there'll be wives to watch husbands distill into dots until they stretch beyond themselves and join the line of the horizon. Children will dream of sleepy kisses on their heads or glance at windowsill ships carved for them on landlocked nights. One or two will open their windows and stare out to sea, brine already salting the blood in their veins.

Someone calls *it's fair to middling*, and a chorus of voices shout *aye*. The men busy themselves with nets and ropes, the women with reassurances: *the water is calm ... the sky clear ... a gentle wind is blowing – all will be well*. They draw themselves in, hold steady and wait.

Lizzie Marshall moves amongst them, exchanges words on weather and the day ahead. She sees Billy Gibbs over by the harbour wall, jumps at the slap of his kit on the deck of The *Flighty Mary*. Pulling her shawl about her face she gets closer, scans the boat, his nets and sees the thinness of the hemp, how in places it has almost worn away to air. Even if he's lucky enough to find those shoals again, she knows these nets will never hold. A fisherman is nothing without good nets. Why hasn't he repaired them? Why has he let them wear so thin? She moves close enough to hear his breath and oh what she would give to feel it over her cheek, her mouth. But there's a North Easterly blowing and it's going to take him out to sea, breath and all.

The luggers leave the shore one by one, tacking out of the little harbour on a lick of wind. This time Billy's the last to go, the tail of the flotilla unfurling in his russet sails like a gash in the sky.

The women of fishing villages are good at waiting; it's in their genes. Over generations they have learnt to divide themselves, rooting their stoicism in harbour walls and cobbled lanes, letting it bed down in the hearths and kitchen stoves of their homes. But their hearts cling to masts and sails, flapping like pennants as they follow their men to the sea. Some, as Lizzie Marshall does, sit by their cottage gates making pillow lace. As they set the bobbins flying the click clack of wood and bone serenades them. Here they can work and bring in extra money, here they can scan the horizon for those little dots of men.

How many times has Lizzie sat watching over the years? Too many and not a word between them, time walling them up with their grievances. Billy will be back on the evening tide and she fears he'll have no catch at all. It's hemp that's needed, that much Lizzie knows, but it comes at a price and there are no spare coins from any purse here.

At dusk the men return, though no one's seen *The Flighty Mary* since she took off round the headland when other boats were making straight for the open sea. As families settle to an easier sleep, the dark of the bay creaks and cranks. It's as if a great leviathan is dragging itself ashore, hauling its body up onto the beach and over the stones. A single light swings in the wind and makes wretched the features of a man already on the brink of despair. He brakes the winch handle, stumbles as he unchains his boat ... tethers her to the shore. He pulls a kerchief from his neck and wipes his bloodied hands as he turns his back on *The Flighty Mary* and walks home.

Lizzy watches his lantern sway until the glow of it has been swallowed by an alleyway. She pulls her shawl tight, holds her lamp low and steps over the chains of the anchored boats. When she reaches *The Flighty Mary* she hovers the beam over the nets: the gaping holes are clear. She puts the lamp on the deck, reaches into her apron pockets and gets to work.

Around the harbour wall young men are murmuring. One of them will have his own boat by the end of the day. Word says Billy Gibbs is dry-docked, no money for hemp to mend his nets and without his nets he's finished. No chasing those phantom shoals of herring now ha, ha. *He's all washed up that Billy Gibbs ... no woman to earn him a shilling.... it's surely the workhouse for him.*

Billy struggles along the drifts of pebbles banked on the beach and when he reaches *The Flighty Mary* cannot bear to look at her, but he must make her ready for sale. The nets are hanging over her side, someone's already been looking her over – vultures the lot of them.

But those nets are not what they were. Startling white thread has filled the gaping holes with panels of close-weave lace, tiny fish shapes stacked along the lie of them. Billy grabs a handful, holds it to his chest and breathes deep to steady himself. He opens his palm watching the lace uncurl, fingers the tiny fish. Such work he knows.

He grips the section in his hands, tugs several times to test its strength and smiles.

Without a word Billy Gibbs makes ready *The Flighty Mary*. He folds her nets in, checks her sails and unfastens her from the buoy. As young men start to swarm on the shore, nodding at their chances, Billy goes over to the winch and starts turning. Already lapping at her sides, the sea slaps her planks with approval and the young men move back. Someone shouts: *I'll make a fair offer, you can trust me Billy Gibbs...* but Billy isn't interested, he's off to the channels – he knows where to find what he's been looking for.

Jacky Taylor has a background in Arts Education and has worked in school, university and community settings. She has an MA in Creative Writing from the University of Chichester and her work has won prizes at Bridport, the Asham Award, the Ilkley Literature Festival, the Momaya Short Story Award and has been shortlisted/longlisted in numerous places as well as published online. She is a member of the Fiction Forge writing collective and a reader/co-editor of their online literary magazine. She finds living by the sea both inspiring and full of surprises.

CHRISTINA SANDERS

Dandelion and Roses

I once told my ex-husband he was a dandelion; a big yellow clock with roots so hardy he could thrive on ashy verges and London gutters without water or sunlight: a Gollum of a plant. No heart. Twelve years later, I was scrubbing scurvy rings from the bath when he called out of the blue, 'Irene,' he said, 'it's high time we met.'

I thought of our sons, tall and serious now, with wives of their own. 'Is this about Benny or Jez?'

That made him laugh – I'd almost forgotten his mad jackal bark; how it turned heads, and jolted babies from sleep – then I remembered how heavily he smoked, 'Oh God, it's not cancer is it?'

That made him laugh again. I held the phone from my ear.

'I'm back, didn't the boys tell you?'

The boys told me Su-Li had left him, flown to Bali with a Dutch financier, her life neatly packed into a set of Louis Vuitton chests. I turned on the cold tap. Water trickled over the white enamel.

'Irene,' he said, 'are you still there?'

Two days later I sat by the lake, where mothers wheeled prams and shouted their children away from the water, dressed in blue jersey – a stab at casual elegance, French nonchalance, though, truth is, my flesh has shrunk with the years, sunk like a soufflé, skin slackened from bone, despite yoga and hours of Pilates. My watch said twelve. Two swans glided over the algae green water. I remembered how my Ex was often late, sometimes by minutes, occasionally hours, or days, as if units of time were elastic and interchangeable and no-one expected them to mean much, anyway. Two boys cycled past, scattering pigeons, and there he was, flying towards me, wild grey hair straggling over his collar, coat unbuttoned, fuchsia lining winking in the wind.

'My God Reeny, how long has it been? Eight or nine years, not a word?'

Reeny? That took me back. 'Twelve,' I said.

'Well, dammit, however many years, you look good, you've done something to your hair...'

His periwinkle blue eyes sparkled with laughter. He shook a cigarette loose from a pack of Camels, cupping his hands around the flame of his lighter. The tip of his cigarette flared red as he sucked in a lungful of smoke, and reached across the backrest, his face solemn now.

'I expect you're wondering why I'm here?'

It's true: I'd often imagined us sitting together, conspiratorial with apology and good intentions – not to argue, carp or slam doors or lapse into silent sulks, help with running the boys to swimming and tennis, family dinners with leafy salads and a clean tablecloth. But the years flew past. I joined a choir and grew baby aubergines in pots. I met Alan in the library where he handled books like precious china, his delicate wrists poking from the sleeves of brushed cotton shirts, suggesting when the Baudelaire was out on loan, I read Verlaine who, he said in his sad, ironic way, was 'more melodic and better with weather.'

The swans dipped their beaks, bobbing white tails to the sky.

'I've been thinking,' my Ex said, 'and it came to me, that in all the to-ing and fro-ing of our divorce, I never knew the reason, I mean the real reason, you divorced me.'

I stared at my boots, now splattered with mud.

I never met Su Li, but the boys showed me pictures of their wedding, her crimson lips and curtain of glossy black hair, pink suede pumps peeping under her silk Pha Nung. Every year they sent the boys cheques, Christmas and birthday cards, exotic with Asian stamps.

'You came all the way from Hong Kong for that?'

He stubbed his cigarette out beneath his shoe; the leather was scuffed bald around the toe. 'You see Irene, what came to me after Su-Li left is that you'd never said it outright, the reason why...'

Across the lake the swans feathered their wings, corrugating the smooth green surface.

'Was it because you thought I was having an affair with Lucy Burton?'

'Lucy who?'

He slapped his thighs. 'You don't remember Lucy Burton?'

'No,' (though how could I forget her 'help me' smile and nipples like ridgepoles; men never understand such women are forged from steel not sugar).

'She lived at number eight. Remember the Wright's Christmas party, when you had to leave early to collect Jez, and I walked her home?'

'No.'

'Well,' he said, 'Was it the time I threw that chair? I had a hellish hangover that day. Or, was it because I missed Bennie's birth? Or because I never helped you get them dressed or got round to putting out the rubbish or mending the loose tiles in the bathroom? Or, those stints in rep, Sheffield, Manchester, Bristol?'

I wiped the mud from my boots with my hankie.

A gust of wind teased up his hair. 'Well, do you remember

that day we took the boys on the river at Barcombe and I lost the oars...?

'Was I there?'

'Irene! Of course you were there, don't you have any memories?' He reached for my hand, drew it to his cheek, skimming my thumb with his fingers. For a moment, the sky tipped off kilter – I remembered the taste of him, a hotel room at Claridges taken on a whim, striding into the lobby, feigning an old Etonian Darling, his pink Oswald Boateng suit too outrageous to dispute – a pearly grey room with a wide crumpled bed; he sang to me from the bath, ice cold glasses of Pouilly Fume never far from our hands.

A small boy in a red anorak knelt at the water's edge, throwing bread over the water; his mother hovered behind, holding his hood.

I shook my hand free, shoved it into my pocket. 'Do you recall a conversation we once had about flowers? I told you, you were a Dandelion.'

'A Dandelion?' He raised his eyebrows theatrically, 'Really? What were you?'

'I wanted to be a rose, one of those rare varieties like *Aunt Bessie* or *Grand Dame*, ruffled and crimson, fragrant as hell...'

He frowned, 'A rose? I'd have had you down as a daisy, or those little pink and white flowers you used to grow in pots in the front garden, Busy something...the ones the cat next door used dig up.'

Through our fifteen years of marriage he had a way of making remarks, which could cut you in two. When challenged, or accused of being thoughtless, he'd simply shrug, 'Why do you have to take everything so seriously...'

The swans swam closer, pecking at the soggy bread lumps. It's a popular misconception that they mate for life. If the pens are barren or elderly, the cobs will abandon them in a flap of a wing to chase a younger female.

I looped my handbag over my shoulder.

'Wait,' he said, 'where are you going? I don't understand. Are you saying we separated because of flowers? That doesn't make sense.'

At the wrought iron gates at the south end of the park, I held out my hand to say goodbye. He looked up from under his straggling fringe, lips pressed together – the same look of wounded outrage he'd perfected playing Lear (or was it Hamlet?), 'his finest triumph' one critic said – then, took my elbow and drew me into his tobacco, his soft cashmere collar which smelt of his citrus cologne.

'I'm not the same person you used to know,' I whispered.

He laughed. Two women at the zebra crossing glanced over. I thought he was going to tell me it wasn't true, we are always the same people but he shook another Camel from the packet.

'A Dandelion, really Irene?'

A familiar snap of irritation stiffened my jaw. I believe life flows in a series of concentric rings, spacious and expansive, dimming the past but, standing in front of the paint crusted gates, his eyes blazing on me, it felt as if time was divided by layers of paper so thin you could look right through them, or rip them to shreds, if you chose.

'Goodbye Daniel.'

He raised his left hand, an ironic salute, turned on his heels, coat tails flapping against his legs.

I walked back along the empty avenue, past shuttered houses and shingle drives, feeling that old itch I could never scratch, prickle once more. Halfway along the road, I heard my Ex shout, 'OK Irene, but one day... one day, I know you'll tell me the real reason we split up, you won't be able to stop yourself.'

I didn't turn round.

Christina Sanders has had short stories and flash fiction published in *Litro, TFM Magazine, Toasted Cheese and Rattletales,* and has performed at Live Lit Events in Sussex. 'Dandelions and Roses' was written after overhearing a conversation about a repentant ex-husband. After several attempts at trying to turn it into a 'story', she consigned it to her laptop's trash bin, but couldn't quite bring herself to press delete. She is currently working on a collection of short stories on the theme of 'Compromise'.

EILEEN MERRIMAN

I Dare You

That Friday, Carrie and I went to the park for the last time. The sun was slipping behind the hills, and the air was thick and balmy. It was early April, and daylight savings had finished, but we didn't want to let go of summer. Not yet.

We sat side-by-side on the swings. I wanted to be higher, faster, more daring than Carrie. So I jumped off the swing, right when it had reached its dizzy peak, and tumbled into the grass below.

'Oh my *God,*' Carrie yelled, 'you're such a kid.'

'You're just jealous,' I called back, without conviction. Being fifteen sucked – not quite a kid, but not quite a woman either. Above me, the dying sun bled into the sky.

Thud. Carrie landed beside me, her school skirt riding up her coppery thighs. Her leather friendship bracelet, the twin of mine, coiled around her shapely ankle. I was jealous of Carrie's perfect skin, her coltish legs, her movie-star name. I was just Jane, plain Jane, the girl no one looked twice at.

That was when I heard it, the low rumble of a car engine. I sat up, squinting at the narrow road running along the side of the park.

'A Porsche,' I breathed, taking in the white convertible with red leather seats and chunky alloy wheels.

'Your dream car.' Carrie scrambled to her feet. 'You should ask for a ride.'

'Whatever. What planet are you on?' The car door opened, and a pair of denimed legs swivelled onto the pavement.

Carrie's lips curled into a smile. 'I dare you.'

I opened my mouth, and then closed it again. Because if I said no, then I was always doomed to be a moon, a colourless moon orbiting Planet Carrie.

'Dare for a dare,' I said, the words falling between us. Leaden. Solid. Irretrievable.

'Dare for a Dare,' Carrie said.

That was how it began.

That was how it ended.

Carrie tugged on my arm.

'He's looking at us.'

'He's not,' I answered. But of course he was, because there was no one else left in the park. The man was leaning against the Porsche, speaking into his phone. Carrie planted her hand in the centre of my back, propelling me forward.

'I dare you,' she repeated.

'I *know*,' I snapped, pushing her hand away.

The man's features became clearer as we drew closer – floppy brown hair, a long face, an aquiline nose. He looked to be in his late thirties, maybe even forty. He lowered his phone, and slipped it into the pocket of his dark blue jeans.

'Nice car,' Carrie said, nudging me.

I dare you.

'Can we have a ride?' I blurted. My face burned in the cooling night air.

The man lifted his chin, and smiled. 'A *ride*?'

'Jane wants a Porsche when she grows up,' Carrie said,

twirling a strand of blonde hair around her finger.

'When she grows up,' he echoed, his eyes travelling over her tightly fitted blouse, the school skirt she'd hitched halfway up her thighs, her gazelle-like ankles. 'Who wants to grow up?'

He stepped to the side, and opened the door.

'You want to ride shot-gun, Jane?'

The interior smelt like mints and leather. I pressed my knees together, watching the road slide beneath the car.

'What's your name?' The man's eyes flicked up to the rear-view mirror. He indicated, and turned left onto the one-way system. The car purred. I wanted to purr too. A Porsche, I was travelling in a Porsche!

Carrie leaned forward, her arms propped up on the backs of our seats.

'Miley.' God, she was such a liar. Miley, what the hell?

He raised an eyebrow. 'As in Miley Cyrus?'

'Yes, like Miley Cyrus.' Carrie sighed. 'If only my parents had called me something normal, like –'

'Like Carrie?' I supplied.

'Yeah, or Jane,' Carrie said, barely hesitating. 'What's your name?'

'William.' He turned the stereo up a notch. 'Do you like The Smiths?'

'The who?' I asked.

Carrie said, 'You must earn lots of money, to drive a car like this.' Her breath smelt like chocolate. William turned his head a fraction. I swear I saw him inhale, saw him breathing in the scent of chocolate-grass-Carrie.

'I'm a businessman,' he said.

'Ugh.' Carrie slumped back into the seat. William chuckled.

'Put your seatbelt on, Miley. I don't want to be responsible for you going through the windscreen, do I?'

I gazed out of the tinted window, watching the familiar sights of Dunedin slide past – the hospital, the university, the tired rows of student flats, the Botanical Gardens. 'Where are we going?'

'State Highway One,' William said. 'You want to go fast, don't you?'

I began to smile. 'Yeah. I want to go fast.'

My memories of the first part of that car ride are glassy, perfect. The way we pressed back into the leather seats as William accelerated up the hill and out of Dunedin, burning off boy racers and SUVs and students in station wagons. The way William sang along to the stereo when 'his' song came on, *William It was Really Nothing*. The way night fell, deep and dark, and it felt as if we were hurtling into the Milky Way.

'Are you hungry, girls?' William asked, after about twenty minutes. I'd texted my mother to say I was spending the night at Carrie's, so she didn't freak out that I hadn't come home yet.

'Starving,' Carrie/Miley said. William slowed and then pulled over. Ten metres ahead of us, an anaemic light-box sign guttered beneath a shop awning: TAKEAWAYS.

'Back soon,' he said, closing the door behind him.

'He didn't even ask us what we want,' Carrie pouted.

I watched the gangly figure slip through the fly screen. 'Maybe we should ask to go home.'

'He's kind of hot, don't you reckon?'

'He's *old*.'

'Older men are sexy. Hey, you should ask to drive. I dare you.'

Twisting in my seat, I narrowed my eyes at her.

'It's your turn, *Miley*. Why'd you give him that stupid name anyway?'

'Oh come on, have some fun, will you?' Carrie took her hair tie out and shook her blonde locks over her shoulders. 'What's my dare, anyway?'

I glanced at the shop, then back at Carrie.

'Think he's sexy, do you?'

Ten minutes later, we sat in the long grass, eating fish and chips by the gibbous glow of the moon. William (call me Will) sat opposite us, his long legs crossed at the ankle.

'Are you married?' Carrie asked.

Will coughed. 'Excuse me?'

'So, you *are* married?'

'No, Miley, I'm not married.' He sounded amused. 'Have you got a boyfriend?'

'No, Will. I don't have a boyfriend,' Carrie said, as if she was playing cat and mouse. I was starting to wonder who was the cat, and who was the mouse.

'Shame.' He nudged my ankle with his foot. 'How about you, Jane? Do you have a boyfriend?'

'No,' I mumbled, shrinking backward.

Carrie yelped. 'Oh my God, something just bit me.'

'A mosquito?' I asked.

'Bigger than that,' she moaned.

Will shuffled towards her. 'Where?'

'My ankle.' Carrie shuddered theatrically.

'Don't think you get white-tailed spiders around her,' Will said. It was hard to see in the grey gloom, but maybe her foot was in his hand. Maybe it was in his lap, even.

'*There,*' Carrie said, as, presumably, he touched the imaginary spot on her ankle.

I dare you.

And yet, I wanted Carrie to succeed in her dare, because maybe then I'd get to fulfil mine. It could be my only chance ever to drive a Porsche.

I stood up. 'I'm going to get my cardigan.'

When I got to the car, I slid into the passenger seat, leaving the door open so the interior light would stay on. That's when I saw the wallet sitting on the driver's seat.

I glanced toward the field. Will's low murmur drifted towards me, followed by a giggle.

Dare for a dare.

I slid out a handful of cards and flipped through them. Credit cards, loyalty cards, a driver's licence –

A driver's licence. I held it up to the light.

James Wilton. DOB 12.09.65. The man in the photo had dark hair, like Will, but that's where the resemblance ended.

What?

For the first time since I'd got in the car, I felt a prickle of unease. I stuffed the cards back in the wallet and threw it on the driver's seat, then scrambled out of the car. There was no murmuring, no giggling anymore – just thick, solid silence.

'Carrie?' My voice wavered.

'If you're looking for Miley, she's answering a call of nature,' Will said behind me. He laughed. 'That made you jump, didn't it?'

'We should go home,' I managed.

'Already?' Will/James said.

Then Carrie/Miley melted out of the gloom and said, 'Thanks Will, my ankle feels sooo much better.'

'I bet it does,' he murmured, walking around to the driver's side.

'We have to go home *right now,*' I hissed.

Carrie looked straight back at me.

'Dare for a dare, Janey. Remember?'

'Just remember,' Will said, once I'd fastened my seatbelt, 'when you put your foot down, this car *goes*, you know what I mean?'

'Uh-huh.' I turned the key in the ignition.

'Her brother's a boy racer,' Carrie said behind us. I wondered if she'd kissed him on the lips. I wondered if she'd opened her mouth.

'Shut up,' I said. Will laughed.

'Are you going to take it out of park? You *have* driven a car before, haven't you?'

Mute, I moved the gear stick back and moved my foot from the brake to the accelerator. The car flew forward.

'Jesus,' Will said, but he didn't sound scared. I was scared out of my brain, scared and exhilarated all at once. Will reached across me to flick on the headlights, but I barely noticed. I was behind the wheel of a *Porsche*, wow, wow, wow.

Carrie leaned over the back of my seat. 'You can go faster than sixty.'

'I *am*.' Seventy, eighty, ninety, one hundred. Wow, wow, wow.

'So what kind of business are you in?' Carrie asked.

'I'm a drug rep,' Will said.

I gripped the steering wheel. 'What sort of drugs?'

He laughed. 'All sorts. I've got some samples, if you're interested.'

'Are you allowed to do that?' Carrie asked.

'I won't tell if you won't. Don't get a speeding ticket, will you, Jane?'

'You're a dealer?' I blurted, barely registering the small town we'd entered and left, all in the space of sixty seconds.

Carrie giggled. 'Like a *drug* dealer?'

That was when I opened my big mouth. I don't know why I said it – maybe because I was sick of Carrie treating me like her kid sister, maybe because I wanted to win the Dare game by calling Carrie's bluff, once and for all.

'Miley wants to try your samples,' I said. 'Don't you, *Miley*?'

After that, I'm not sure what actually happened and what was just a figment of my adrenaline-swamped, drug-addled brain.

Another field. Carrie asking Will what was in the pipe. Will saying, trust me, Miley, this will blow your mind. Carrie, inhaling and turning to me: I dare you. Me, insisting: I don't want to play the game anymore.

Will: do you like fast, Jane? Come on, you don't want to miss out, do you? *I dare you, Jane.*

The sweetest rush, exploding into my brain. The stars, whirling overhead, faster and faster. The mercurial heaviness, spreading through my limbs. The dew, soaking into the back of my clothes. Will saying, *I dare you Carrie,* over and over, as if he'd known her real name all along. The hands on my belly and the mouth on mine, Carrie's or Will's or both, I don't know, and then –

And then they were gone.

There's a leather bracelet I keep in the top drawer of my dresser. I don't deserve to keep it, but I can't throw it away either. Sometimes, when my chest feels so tight I can hardly breathe, I slip it over my wrist and curl into bed. But when I close my eyes it's Will's voice I hear, worming into my brain.

I dare you.

I don't know where they went. After the starry blur, and the hands and the mouths and, oh God, I don't know what I did or they did and I don't want to know, I don't – after that, the next clear memory I have is of the sun searing the backs of my eyelids and the lowing of cows. My mouth was dry, and my head felt as if it was about to split open. I thought I was losing my mind.

I didn't lose my mind. I lost Carrie.

The police never found her. They found the Porsche, the stolen Porsche, abandoned in an empty field a hundred kilometres away from the spot where I woke up, disorientated and alone. They didn't find Will, or any man matching his description.

I used to worry that Carrie was dead, but there are fates worse than death.

Sometimes I even dare to wonder who won the game.

Eileen Merriman's awards include coming second in the 2015 Bath Flash Fiction Award, being commended in the 2015 Bath Short Story Award and coming third in the 2014 and 2015 Sunday Star Times Short Story competitions. Her work has previously appeared in a number of journals and anthologies, including *Smokelong Quarterly, The Island Review, Literary Orphans,* the *2015 Bath Short Story Anthology*, the *Sunday Star Times, F(r)iction, Takahe, Headland* and *Flash Frontier*. Her young adult novel, *Pieces of You,* will be published in 2017 (Penguin Random House). More information can be found at her website: eileenmerriman.co.nz

RHIANNON BULL

Though the Waves Toss

I want you to imagine yourself in your favourite place, says Amy's counsellor.

Much as Amy would like to be somewhere else right now, Amy doesn't really think she needs to be seeing the school counsellor, and she's absolutely sure that imagining she's in her favourite place isn't going to change the fact that her best friend Freya isn't here anymore. Instead of imagining her favourite place, Amy just takes a sip of her coke.

It's so stiflingly hot today that the can is already warm, and the sticky, sugary drink is just making her thirstier, but Amy drinks it anyway. She's bought it now, after all. She's bought her counsellor "call me Jackie" a can of coke too, but she notices that she hasn't touched it, even though Amy opened them both when she got here.

Aren't you thirsty, she asks call-me-Jackie, but call-me-Jackie just tells her to try not to transfer her worries about Freya to the can of coke, and please can she try to imagine herself in her favourite place? Where has she visited recently? Has she been anywhere that made her feel calm?

Transference (in German *Übertragung*): From Freudian psychoanalysis; the redirection of emotions towards an unconnected object.

Amy read about Freud when Freya was studying him in her A-Level Psychology class. Only it turned out that hardly anyone thinks that Freudian theory is credible any more. When she'd mentioned this to Freya, Freya had just said that her Psychology teachers didn't seem to like him much either, so Amy still doesn't really understand why they are teaching Freud in Psychology classes. She wonders whether call-me-Jackie likes Freud.

You could try closing your eyes if that helps? Call-me-Jackie suggests helpfully.

Amy hopes she doesn't like Freud. And anyway, she'd only bought her a coke to be polite.

Amy?

Amy shrugs, and tells call-me-Jackie that she doesn't think that closing her eyes will help, and what does she think of Freud?

We're not here to talk about me, Amy. Now would you try just humouring me for a minute, and close your eyes? Trust me, this will really help you when you need to calm down.

Amy takes another sip of coke, and wishes that she hadn't bothered to buy a can for her counsellor, but she closes her eyes anyway. It feels strange, sitting there with her eyes closed and knowing that someone else is in the room. She doesn't like the feeling that her counsellor is still looking at her. Who knows what she looks like with her eyes closed?

Now I want you to imagine you're in a calm place, call-me-Jackie says, encouraged that Amy has shut her eyes.

What calm place? Amy asks.

Well, where have you been recently? Have you been anywhere that made you feel really happy? Or do you have a favourite place you could imagine yourself in?

Amy's favourite place is the hidden ledge partway down the riverbank. It's difficult to get to because the banks are very steep and it involves a lot of clutching at roots to stop yourself from sliding down through slick, dark mud to the river. She only knows about it because Freya showed her where it was. She doesn't know how Freya discovered it. But Amy can't tell her counsellor about that place, because if people thought that might be where Freya was when she fell, then Amy wouldn't be able to go there anymore, and really that's the only place that she can go to be alone and pretend that Freya is still here.

Amy tries to think of somewhere else she's been recently that made her happy, but the only new places she has been to in the last few months are the gardens and the parks and the National Trust properties that her mum keeps dragging her to at the moment. Every time they go on one of these trips, Amy is uncomfortably aware that her mum thinks these will do her good, and that she's hoping that Amy will open up to her in one of these places. Only she can't. It's still too hard.

In the end Amy decides to lie, and tells her counsellor that her favourite place is in Cornwall. She's just read *Rebecca* and watched the Alfred Hitchcock adaptation with her mum the other weekend, and she'd thought Cornwall looked nice so she supposes it is almost true.

Great! Call-me-Jackie is more cheerful now, relieved that Amy seems to be in a compliant mood and that things are going the way they're supposed to again. Even with her eyes closed, Amy can tell that call-me-Jackie is delighted that Amy is doing as she's told. She wonders whether counsellors ever get any counselling themselves.

Okay Amy, I want you to imagine yourself in that place in Cornwall, call-me-Jackie says. Try and imagine that you're really *in* that place. I'll give you a minute to picture it.

Even though most of the film is set in the house, Amy imagines that she is on the beach, by Rebecca's stone cottage. She likes the idea of having a little cottage like that, a space that's her own; of owning a boat which she can use to escape whenever she would like to. She imagines that she is there now, digging her toes into the wet sand, with the sea behind her and the house in front of her. The cottage is built into the rocks, with steps leading up and around the back of the house to the top of the cliffs. No – actually, she scrubs out those steps. She decides that the only way to get here is by boat. Amy tilts her head upwards until the back of her neck hurts, looking up and up to the top of the cliffs, where knotted plants curl and tumble back down to where she's stood on the beach. She doesn't know the names of plants that grow near the sea, but she thinks that these would be too far away for her to see from the beach, anyway.

Now, Amy, call-me-Jackie interrupts. In the scene you're in, what colours are standing out?

Amy pauses.

Well, it's in black and white.

What do you mean?

Rebecca is in black and white. The film I mean. Not the book, obviously.

Call-me-Jackie is confused.

Why are you imagining Rebecca?

That's where I am – where I'm imagining I am. Do you know the film? I'm at the cottage, by the beach.

There's a moment in which neither of them speak, while Amy's counsellor tries to work out what to say and Amy wonders why the colours are so important. Eventually call-me-Jackie tries again.

Can you imagine the beach in colour, Amy?

Amy tries. She imagines the plants turning green, the sand brightening to yellow, and the blue-grey of the sea. She turns the sky blue, too, and the cliffs dark grey, but then she tries to colour in the cottage and she gets stuck. She's never actually been to Cornwall. What colour would the cottage be? Amy can only imagine lines of whitewashed houses when she thinks of

Cornwall, which doesn't help – unless the cottage would be painted white, too? She doesn't remember the cottage looking like it was painted in the film... Hang on, she needs to think about this for a minute.

Amy eventually gives up trying to guess, and keeps the stone cottage in the monochrome of the film. This makes it harder to believe she's really there, but she supposes it's enough to keep call-me-Jackie happy.

Most of it's in colour now, she assures her counsellor.

Call-me-Jackie gives Amy a damp smile, and asks if she can please carry on imagining the scene, then. What can you smell? She prompts Amy. What can you hear? I want you to tell me whatever pops into your head first – try not to think about it too much. Just let it come to you. Like a daydream.

The dreamwork (in German *Traumwerk)*: The transference of unconscious thoughts (the latent content) into the representations of a dream (the manifest content).

Amy knows that Freud thought that you could interpret dreams, that they revealed things about a person that they couldn't admit to themselves. She's convinced now that call-me-Jackie needs to reconsider her therapeutic methods, but, for some reason that definitely has nothing to do with Freud, Amy is surprised to find that she is enjoying imagining the scene from Rebecca. So she carries on.

There's a salt-wind in the air, she tells call-me-Jackie. And there's seaweed drifting back and forth in the fringes of the waves, and that smells of salt, too. When I stand by the cottage I can smell the heat of sun on stone. I can hear the susurrus of the waves as they unbraid across the beach, and the clink and rattle of the boat. And I can hear seagulls, all laughing at each other as they wheel in cool puffs of air high above me.

This is great, Amy, call-me-Jackie tells her. Those are some great details. And now, she says, conspiratorially, this is important Amy. Do you think you can keep this place just to yourself?

Amy considers this. She supposes that sounds okay – she's not sure why she would need to tell anyone else that she has been imagining *Rebecca*.

It could be somewhere that's just for you, call-me-Jackie continues. Somewhere you can go, when you need to. Somewhere, she suggests tentatively, that perhaps you could even keep from Freya?

Amy notices again that call-me-Jackie hasn't taken even a sip of her coke, and it strikes her, now, that it really isn't very nice for call-me-Jackie to just forget about it, when Amy went to the trouble of buying it for her. She didn't have to bring her a coke. She's annoyed that call-me-Jackie just keeps making her think about Freud all the time, without even drinking the coke that Amy's brought her, and as she grows more and more annoyed thinking about this, Amy can feel mucus building up at the back of her nose and fat, hot tears waiting to roll from her eyes. But she doesn't cry. She's been practising hard at not-crying. So Amy just keeps her eyes closed and tries to look pensive, as if she's thinking seriously about call-me-Jackie's suggestion.

Only Amy knows that she isn't doing that at all. She won't ever keep her friend out of any part of her life, and in her imagination she takes the little boat by Rebecca's stone cottage, pushes it out into the vast ocean, and goes to find Freya.

Amy hears the toss and slap of the water against her legs, feels the sudden lurch as she pushes herself off the beach and scrambles into the boat. It doesn't matter that she doesn't know how to sail, because the boat is tugged along by the current, dragging her away from the shore until the beach and the cottage are a distant blur behind her and she's floating out into the flat, empty sweep of the sea. It's still hot, and the sun dries the saltwater on Amy's skin so that it feels pinched and tight and she's left with a fine white crust over her legs. Like icing sugar. She leans over the side of the boat and dips one hand into the sea so that her fingers grow cold and look pale, and leave their own tiny slipstream behind them as they cut through the water.

The little boat glides lazily through the water, bright and still on this baking summer day. Amy lies back on the rough wood, feeling the sun seeping into her skin. Occasionally the water breaks against the boat and droplets spatter over Amy's legs and the deck, briefly leaving cool speckles on her skin and dark smudges on the boat before the water evaporates again. The sea is dazzling, the sun glinting off the tips of the waves in brilliant white flashes. With the boat sitting low in the water, it seems to Amy that there is nothing left in all the world but the sea and the sky and the space in between, and she is lost in the middle of it.

As Amy drifts through the saltwater and the seaweed and the surf, she suddenly notices something else moving through the waves. The boat moves closer, and Amy sees that it's a person, tiny and dark against the water. And then Amy realises that it's Freya, that she hasn't drowned at all but was just swept so far along the river that she's made it out to sea and that's why no one's found her yet, and Amy pulls her up into the boat and she and Freya go sailing across the ocean forever. And Amy knows then that she's finally found a place that makes her feel calm.

Rhiannon Bull is a writer and illustrator currently based in the muddy, marshy Essex countryside. She is interested in the relationship between people and place, and in exploring the landscapes, languages and mythologies that form these relationships. She is still enjoying just starting out as a fiction writer, the freedom to experiment that this allows, and seeing her first few publications come to be. More information can be found at www.rhiannonbull.com

SARA COLLINS

Light Like You

I was science mad back then. I was lying on my bed – shirt off, Converse on the floor, damp socks shoved into them – thinking about dark matter, about the impossibility of feeling something that passes through you without the slightest disturbance, without even the tiniest trace, when the bell rang.

A man I'd never seen before at the door. Hair high and frantic, a million tiny arms waving. Blue shell suit, white Nikes, a packet of B & H in one hand, and a T-shirt that read 'Smoking Kills'. On the street behind him, three buses in a row hissed away from the stop. A moment of silence pressed itself between us. I snapped out of it.

'Black Panthers? Around the corner, breds. Just take the first left and then straight back a couple decades. Your hair'll be right at home.'

'You must be Elroy.'

'I must be.'

'I'm your father.'

'I know.'

I'd been up since two that morning, back and forth to the

toilet, so I wasn't in the mood for meeting anybody, let alone the Prodigal Dad.

All week there'd been the hot shimmer off the tarmac, the low clouds as slow and swollen as cows. So hot we'd barely had energy for keepy-up. Most days we cut through the park to Digger's, because Digger's mother was usually too far gone to take any notice of fag ends piled into coffee cups in his bedroom, or the lager on our breath. We hardly ever came back to mine, only when things were a real state of emergency at his place. He could sense it beforehand, the way some people's bones ache before it even looks like rain. He'd get going about what he 'had to put up with', like the night he fed his mother canned dog food and she just gobbled it all up with a wry, diluted smile before passing out. When I argued that surely this was *him* abusing *her,* he'd chuckle and tell me I had no clue.

The heat pawed at us. But the feverish days gave way eventually to skies that went slowly pinkish then dark as throats. I'd look up as if it had taken me by surprise, the nightfall, and say, aw'right blood, see you tomorrow and Digger would give me a nod, yeah man tomorrow.

'So, Elroy, eh? Heh-heh. You gunna let me in?'

My father's face was scored with fine scars. And he was light. Very light. But this I'd already heard many times by then from Nana Iris, when I asked her about him: *'You bloodclot father a lightskin', good for nothing, pretty-eye chancer, a true-born cocksman. Is him you favour, Elroy. And watch out. Girls can't get enough of that kinda chap, you mother included.'*

'My mother said you were in prison.'

'Did she? She mussa been wishing I was.'

'I think she was wishing you were dead.'

He pointed at me and winked and chuckled, like an American politician fake-spotting a friend in a crowd. 'You not gunna let me in? You suppose to be expecting me.'

I noticed then that there was a small boy behind him, clutching a brown paper bag. Thin, blinking, wearing knock-off trainers, the kind that flashed like a slot machine when he walked. My father glanced behind him, as if he'd just noticed the boy as well.

'This? This your brother Job.'

'Did you really name him *Job*?'

'His mama did.'

The pong on him as he pushed past me towards the kitchen: sweet yet sharp, something decayed but disinfected. Old Spice and fruit cups. The smell of blood and hospitals and drunks.

The boy stopped at the threshold, held out his hand. He was a weighed-down comma of a kid.

'Job.'

'So your father said.'

'He's your father as well, isn't he?'

'In name only.'

We found them in the kitchen, our father herding my mother into the sink, his face as serious as a toddler's.

'You mother still a fine woman, Elroy. She was the talk of Maypen back in her day.'

She spooned up yesterday's stew, held the pot to her chest and blushed against her dark skin, like this was some kind of country dance and he was some kind of suitor instead of the no good son of a bitch who'd already left her high and dry. 'Don' mind you father, Elroy. He talking foolishness, just cos he hasn't clapped eyes on me in years.'

'This is Job,' my father said. The boy offered his hand.

'Job?' Her brows arched into question marks.

'*His* son,' I said.

'Oh. We were only expecting you, Victor. But. Always room for one more!'

Our father flicked a finger at me and barked, 'Marcia, wha' the bloodclot wrong wid this boy? He a sissy?'

'I'm not!'

'Not what?'

'A sissy,' I said, which only made me seem like one.

'Well, so *you* say,' he replied, belching, and lighting a fag.

Mum giggled, and so did Job, a high-pitched wheezing.

'You see these two red nigger?' our father said, pointing to me, then himself, with the fag. 'Two *men* right here! Real bloodclot men. And don' you forget it.'

'He light like you Victor for true. I always saying is a shame he not a girl. He would have that good hair from you, too, but at least he light like you.'

'Marcia, I been saved,' our father said. He clicked his fingers and Job pulled something out of his bag: a King James Bible. This made me want to laugh harder than anything that had happened since I'd let them in. 'I been washed by His blood and I come to make amends. To you, to the boy.'

'Preacher said he must!' Job piped up.

'I come to make you an offer of –'

'He's come to put it right!' Job kicked his feet, bouncing the bag on his lap.

' – marriage.'

'No,' I said, laughing. 'No, no, no. What about *his* mother?' I pointed at Job.

'My mother's dead.'

'Oh,' I said.

'*She's* to be my new one,' Job said, pointing at my mother.

My mother always dressed for the sort of occasion least likely to happen to her: bridal satin or disco neon, as if her clothes were living the kind of life she aspired to. *Dressing Jamaican,* Digger called it. She looked lost amidst the crew of sensibly dressed Polish ladies she cleaned houses with. That morning was no exception: ripped green denim, a T shirt with a cartoon character on it, gold sandals, a green streak in her fringe and enormous gold hoops in her ears, wearing a beatific smile that did not match her outfit: the smile of a saint, the smile of a woman being confronted for the first time in sixteen years by the man who'd ditched her and her belly almost as soon as the plane had touched down in the promised land she'd left sweet breezes and soft water for. And that man's son.

'The lamb of God takes away the sins of the world,' my father said, and my mother said, 'Amen.'

His tongue pecked at his bottom lip. 'In the life of the Spirit, we *all* lambs. *Re-gifted* with innocence, whitened, yes, *purified* like cleaned wool, but –'

'Sacrificial,' I said.

Our father turned to me with a doggedly benevolent expression. He started to sing, *'On a hiiii-i-iill, far aaaaa-way! Stood an o-ho –old rugged cross…'*

'You can still sing, Victor,' my mother said.

'Hymns only, Sister Marcia! And I go by Brother Vic now, Sister Marcia.'

'*She* is just plain Marcia,' I said.

'Plain Marcia!' Job squealed, swinging his legs. Our father cuffed him on the shoulder.

'Preach something for them, Son,' our father said to Job, nodding at the Bible. 'Go on.' To the rest of us he said, 'Watch this.'

It was like watching a wind-up doll. Job stood and closed his eyes. The only sound was the quiet rattle of his chest and the ticking of Mum's old oven. He raised a hand; his little palm flashed bright against his cocoa-coloured skin. He screwed up his face, he moaned and pursed his lips into an Oh. He started to shake, from the knees up. He bounced, and rocked back and forth, and tossed his head. And the words, when they came, seemed to bubble up from his gut to his throat, quickly, carelessly, like a function of his body that he couldn't control. '*This* is the dayyyyy-uh. The Lordddd has made-uh.'

Our father called out, 'Hallelujah!'

'*His* hands are on them-uh, he will bless them and sanctify them-uh, he will favour them with income streams, he will fill their cups till they run over, he will shine his mercy upon them he will fill them with the Spirit he will make his face to shine upon them he will prime the pump of their wellbeing and give them financial salvation he-will-bless-them-abundantly-Hallelujah! Oh Lord, thank you for Jesus… thank *you* for Jesus.'

'Hallelujah!' our father exclaimed.

My mother fetched a glass of water. Job gulped it down, watching me out of the corner of his eye. I began to wonder who the real swindler was, between the pair of them.

Our father asked my mother if he could have a word, in private.

According to Job, they'd been on the road for a time with something that sounded like a church-cum-cult called the Apostles' Way, sleeping at caravan parks until they'd left theirs in a long term parking facility just off the M25. Job had achieved some fame already as a kid preacher and because of the re-enactment he and our father did of Abraham's intended sacrifice of Isaac.

He'd livened up after our father left the room, but now we were both pretending we couldn't hear the whispers and intermittent gasps coming from down the hall. I wanted to put my fingers in my ears. Job fished into his bag again and pulled out an old Essence magazine – Grace Jones on the front, and 'Dare to be You!' in attention-seeking yellow letters -- and began to thumb through it. Outside, the buses lunged at the sidewalk. A sudden gust kicked up the oak leaves by the front door. I pictured Digger, in the park without me, probably stretched out on the seesaw with a loaded bagel and a Freezee slurp. I was missing all of that. For this.

The shout seemed to come from far away, through a long tunnel: 'Out! Get out!' I ran out without thinking. My mother's hair was hanging around her shoulders like a torn down curtain.

'Okay, Marcia,' our father was saying. 'Okay. Settle down. If you only just t'ink about it –'

'I said out!'

Job asked no questions. He took up his bag, the Bible and our father by the hand. Together they went out to the bus stop, where our father looked from the street to our house, and Job sat beside him swinging his blinking feet.

It's ordinary matter scientists have worked for centuries to understand, the things we can see and touch and hold. Ordinary matter squeaks and whines, wagging its tail and knocking things over, while dark matter – ubiquitous, uninterested, feline – is the biggest secret the Universe has ever kept.

But the known world is constructed as much by the laws of memory as by the laws of light. Any kind of matter can lie just outside the reach of memory, where it becomes a metaphor for the loss of faith, the embodiment of nothing.

It's been many years. I heard tell once that they had taken their show on the road again, but I have never seen our father or Job again.

That winter, when it came, my mother bought a grey coat. She stopped talking about going home one day, began to swear in Polish around the house. But that night, she stood at the kitchen window and watched the buses pulling away until the sun dropped lower and lower in the darkening sky. 'He only wanting money,' she said. 'After all this time. Bastard.' She spat into the sink. And the sun set, finally, on the only day all summer that I'd spent apart from Digger.

Later, I left Mum in bed and jogged to Digger's, through the shortcut between the flats, rubbish bins lined up casual as lookouts, graffiti blistered along the walls. It was a silent night. I stopped just at the entrance to the park, snagged on my own thoughts. A streetlamp stuttered on and off at the far side, and I stood beside the swings and watched. It seemed almost a cry for help, some kind of broken Morse code. The flickering light gave a kind of pulse to the night so that the park seemed to be waiting there with me or *for* me, and suddenly there came without warning an answering pulse in me, hammering just beneath my breastbone: one quick hard knock after another pounding into me so I could barely catch my breath.

Sara Collins studied law at the London School of Economics and worked as a lawyer for seventeen years. She is a final year student for the Master of Studies in Creative Writing at Cambridge University, where she was the recipient of the 2015 Michael Holroyd Prize for Re-creative Writing. Her work has been published in the *2015 Bath Short Story Award Anthology* and in *The Caribbean Writer.* She is working on her debut novel, *Frannie Langton,* which was shortlisted for the 2016 Lucy Cavendish Fiction Prize. Twitter: @mrsjaneymac